THE ETERNAL SMILE

D0761782

By the same Author

*

BARABBAS

THE DEATH OF AHASUERUS

THE DWARF

THE MARRIAGE FEAST

PILGRIM AT SEA

THE SYBIL

THE HOLY LAND

MARIAMNE

THE ETERNAL SMILE

THREE STORIES BY

PÄR LAGERKVIST

HILL AND WANG, NEW YORK

Translation © Chatto & Windus 1971
All rights reserved
ISBN (paperback edition) : 0–8090–1358–4
ISBN (cloth edition) : 0–8090–4309–2
Library of Congress catalog card number: 78–145810
First American edition June 1971
Manufactured in the United States of America
2 3 4 5 6 7 8 9 0

CONTENTS

ACKNOWLEDGEMENT

Acknowledgement is due to Messrs Jonathan Cape Ltd for permission to reprint the translations by Erik Mesterton and Denys W. Harding of THE ETERNAL SMILE and GUEST OF REALITY.

The Eternal Smile

THERE were once upon a time a few of the dead sitting together somewhere in the darkness. They didn't know where—perhaps nowhere. They were sitting and talking to pass eternity away.

"No," said one of them, continuing a conversation that had been going on for ages on end, "the living are too self-complacent. They busy themselves with their odds and ends and imagine they're alive. When they come out of their houses in the morning and hurry off in the sharp air, pleased with a new day, they shoot secret glances at each other as much as to say, 'You and I, we live.' And they hurry off to their works, good and bad, heap them on top of each other, one above the other, till the whole thing topples over and they can begin again. They're conceited, contented little insects, nothing more. They build up and pull down, build up and pull down, and sweat with zeal and wink secretively at one another. 'We live, we live, we live.' They build and build, and they point to everything they've got half-finished or near enough. 'We've got all this done, every bit of it.' They're conceited little insects, nothing more."

He sat staring in front of him, fretting. He was lean, embittered, tormented.

"Up to the present, life has a few million millions dead," he went on. "It is we who live. We exist in those below. We exist quietly. We go about in stockinged feet; no one hears us. It is not we who make the fuss; we are unobtrusive and silent. It is not we who mind steam engines, who start trains, who call up on the phone. But it is we who live. It is not we who build up and pull down, build up and pull down. It is not we who feel that this is morning, that this is evening. But it is we who live."

And he sighed heavily.

"It is we who think of everything, who arrange everything; it is we who cannot forget anything. It is we who long for everything, day after day, year after year, for thousands and thousands of years.

"Whenever there is a little quiet, it is us. When anyone weeps, it is us. Whenever anything really happens, it is us.

"The living is simply what is dead."

He stopped short and spat in front of him. Wiping his mouth, he mumbled something to himself which no one could hear.

"I wonder whether you are right, after all," rejoined another, mildly and reflectively. "God knows whether we are so important.

"I wonder whether, if one looks deeper, the living, too, haven't some significance. They make use of us, they exploit us unscrupulously, and with it all they brag so much about themselves. But they do really contribute something of their own. And such as it is it has great value at the moment, even though later on it has hardly any. I can't agree that they haven't a certain importance of their own. I even venture so far as to maintain that it is they who live and we who are dead."

They sat silent a long while, each turning it over in his own mind.

At last the lean one began again, resting his head in his dry hand and staring out into what looked like darkness.

"It is long since I was alive, but I remember that I lived by the sea. I believe that I was born there and stayed there all the time. But possibly I only came there once by chance and left again. I no longer remember, and anyhow it makes no difference. In any case, I remember that I lived by the sea.

"I remember the small rattling pebbles at the water's edge. But the gale above all, drowning the other noises, the roaring gale, with all the great clouds over the water. And I remember the quietness, the unmoving quietness, the complete silence around me.

"The sea, that is the only great thing down there. Down there it is eternity. I lived by the sea. I had a house close to the shore with a view over the unfathomable depths. In one of the windows stood a little dried pot plant which I always forgot to water. I don't know why I remember it; it played no part in my life. I lived by the sea. Yet I remember it very well. I remember that it was still there when I was going to die, and how I thought to myself, if it were not that I was going to die I ought to get up and give it a little water. I recall, too, that as I lay and looked at it I thought it strange that it should outlive me. Poor thing. However, it played no part in my life. I lived by the sea.

"I was a man of great importance. As far as I know there was no one in my time like me and no one so important. At least I never noticed it. I didn't meet other people very much either. I lived alone by myself. I listened to the gale and to the quietness. I was already in my lifetime a living, struggling man. I felt within myself everything that really is. I was greater and more than anybody else. In point of fact, so far as I know, there was no one besides myself.

"I was simply made to die. That is not true of everyone, of course. But I had the proper dignity and weight. Living really consisted in me. I could die secure. I needed only to die."

He left off. A deep sigh forced itself from his lips.

Then he went on, seriously as before.

"I think that in order to be dead—that is, in order to belong to eternity—one needs to be something really important. One needs to have been outside and above life in the ordinary sense, not to have been included in it. And I was, as I have already said, a very important man."

The second now joined in.

"Without going into what has just been said, I should like to mention that I, too, was a very important person, though it is with the greatest reluctance that I say it of myself. I was—if not in my own, yet in everyone else's eyes—the most remarkable person who had existed on the earth up to that time. I lived a rich, glorious life; I carried out feat after feat, one great work after another, which mankind will never be able to forget. I myself, however, have forgotten what it was all about. And even if I could recall all that, it would only weary me here. I don't feel in the least remarkable now. I feel very ordinary, strangely insignificant.

"I was simply made to live. To my mind anyone is fit for sitting here and being dead. But for living, really living, and taking pleasure in it, only the great, the prodigious man, is fit for that. I was such a man. In my own and many others' view it was not intended that I should ever die. And, in fact, it came about through a trivial accident."

He sighed, he too, and sat mute for a long time, sunk in his thoughts. Then he added, "As I have already mentioned, I was a very exceptional man. However, I am not remarkable now.

"I think life is something incomprehensibly great and rich. I think death is nothing. Despising my own emptiness, I love everything living.

"Nevertheless, I would maintain that very few people have really lived. Although I am reluctant to speak about myself, I should like to mention that, so far as I know, I alone have lived.

"However, I am dead now."

He left off. It seemed as if the conversation were at an end.

But it was continued by a third person. He was a fat,

thick-set man with little eyes, and his hands clasped across his expansive paunch. He looked like a grocer, trustworthy but a little undistinguished, perhaps. His short legs hung dangling in what looked like darkness. You could see that if he had been sitting on a chair his feet would not have reached the floor. He said, "Although I haven't understood anything of what you gentlemen have been saying, I feel all the same how completely I agree with you about everything.

"How good it was to be alive. How great life was, and how lovely. When I stood behind my counter with all my goods around me, with the smell of cheese and coffee, of soft soap and margarine, how good life was.

"My shop was the biggest in the town. As far as I know there was no other so important as mine. It was in the best street; everybody came to me. I had choicer goods than any other. Yes, so far as I know there was no other.

"I am not saying it to appear important. I was quite an ordinary person after all. I was Mr Pettersson, the grocer, nothing more. I was like everybody else. I was Mr Pettersson, the grocer. But I thank God that I have lived.

"It was hard when I had to die. I turned to the wall and said to myself, this is the end, Pettersson. I couldn't believe that it wasn't the end of everything. There had been no time for me to think about higher matters; I had had enough to do with my own. I was no remarkable person, either. I was Mr Pettersson, the grocer. I was like everybody else. And when I lay and thought back over my life, when I thought how year in and year out I had stood and weighed out groceries and wrapped up salt herring, then I thought it was too strange if on that account I should exist through all eternity. I said to myself, damned if I know whether there's any life after death; I don't think there is. Then I died.

"And yet there was, after all! Here I sit, after all. And it's as though nothing had happened; it's as though I still stood and weighed out groceries and wrapped up herring. I am still Mr Pettersson, the grocer."

He left off, moved. Then he added, "Although I don't understand anything, I am thankful for everything. I have lived. I am dead. All the same I live. I am thankful for it all."

He stopped and sat there sunk in deep thought.

It grew quiet.

The conversation passed on upward in the darkness to other groups of people, farther and farther removed; it went on in a loop, which rose higher and higher. Then it twisted downward again. After nearly a hundred years it once more reached the group where it had started. It came in now from the opposite side. But this time it didn't give rise to so many words.

The embittered one said, "As I mentioned before, I was a very important man. I believe, too, that in order to be dead—that is, in order to belong to eternity—it is necessary to be something really important. It is necessary to have been outside and above life in the ordinary sense, not to have been included in it. I was such a man."

The second one spoke next. "I think that life is everything. I think that life is something incomprehensibly great and rich which can only be grasped by the great man, the prodigious man. I was such a man. However, I am dead now."

Then the grocer, who sat a little out of the way and apart from them, added, "I am still Mr Pettersson, the grocer."

But while they just sat thinking about this, other conversations were going on among the people round about them; everyone was describing his life, absorbed in it.

One said, "I am thinking about myself and my life.

"My workshop, where I worked from morning till night, lay on the outskirts of a big town. I was a locksmith, I did nothing else; what I am going to tell you is about that. The little smithy, where I was always by myself—for I wouldn't have any help or anyone about—lay hidden away in an orchard where there were many trees and a lot of fruit and flowers, which someone whom I didn't know had planted some time long ago. But everything was unkempt and ran wild; I had my own job, I did nothing else. I stood in the half-dark smithy from morning till late into the night and made my locks for all the houses that people lived in, away in the town.

"I didn't make them in the ordinary way; I made every one different. I made them so that each one was different from every other that there was, and could only be opened by somebody who had the one key and knew the way to turn it in the lock; for I made them so that the key had first to be turned in one direction, then pushed farther in and turned in the other; or I would devise other secret methods. I thought out hidden subtleties which only one person could master. I hated people. I shut them in each by himself. My locks became famous. They were sold in a shop, but I don't know where it was. I didn't know the town, I never left my house, I worked at my own job. Everyone wanted my locks for their houses, so that no one should be able to break in. I worked day and night, I stood bent over my work year in and year out, alone, I worked at my own job, I made locks, the money piled up. They were expensive locks; people bought them all the same. I was rich, I didn't know what I owned, I was poor. I grew old and grey, my fingers began to shake at their work; I was alone, no one saw it; I went back over things in my mind, I went on working with my shaking hands. I am telling you about my life.

"Then it happened one morning when I raised my head and looked out of the dusty workshop window that through a gap in the orchard I saw a young girl go past on the road. She was seventeen perhaps, perhaps eighteen, she was walking bareheaded, she had fair hair that shone in the sun, she was happy and looked about her as she walked. It was only for a minute that I had a sight of her; then she was gone, hidden by the trees.

"I stood gripped by something. I dropped my work and stared out, but she was no longer there. The picture remained, her fair hair, her happy face, which was so young and firm. I thought I knew her. I had never seen her before; I never saw people. I felt as if she had been my child, I don't know why. I had never lived with any woman. I, miserable old man, bent and shaking, I felt as if she were my child. Her hair was so fair that the sun when it came and caressed it seemed to linger there. I didn't know who she was. I only knew I loved her. I stood staring out, but she was no longer there.

"Slowly I turned back again to my work. My hands shook more than before. No one saw it, only I. I found it hard to hold the parts; I tightened my hold of them, I turned back again; I drew my rough hand across my mouth, I got ready to go on with my own job. I said to myself, there is nothing to love, nothing is worth our love, nothing. I turned back again, blotted it out. I worked at my own job. But my eyes had grown so dim; I went and wiped the dust from the window, so that I could see to work. I waited for her to go the same way back again.

"The whole day went by. I worked hard, I got more done that day than usual. Not before evening when the light began to fail did she come back.

"I saw her again. She went along smiling. What was left of the sun shone in her hair alone. I stood mute at the window and gazed.

"When she had vanished I crept out. I went through the orchard. It was summer, there was a smell of flowers; but everything had grown wild. I came out onto the road. It was all strange. I crept after her. I came into the town, I followed her at a distance, the streets opened out one after the other, I saw nothing but her. She went into a house. I stood outside, but a long way off. The children began to laugh at me—I had my apron on. Slowly I went back to my own place.

"Now I thought no more about her. I went on working, as before. In a little while I grew very old. Summer came to an end and autumn set in. The leaves began to fall in the orchard. Then one night it happened that while I stood as usual bent over my work my heart went empty and cold. I was so cold that I shivered; my whole body was like ice. I dropped what I was working on. I was shaking. My legs wouldn't carry me; I felt as if I couldn't live much longer. Such an anguish came upon me that I looked around me wildly in the half-dark room where only a lantern spread its flickering light. It was windy and raining outside; the overgrown trees beat against the panes with their bare branches. I didn't want to die, not alone, not here where everything was my own. I staggered out into the passage. I pushed open the door, went out. The wind tried to knock me down; the rain beat against my face. I gathered all the strength I had left. I staggered out onto the road, into the town.

"There was no one in the bleak wind-swept streets, only me. I groped my way in the rain and darkness. I went groping my way to her house; I wanted to die near her, near my child. I couldn't find it, I went wrong. At last I got there. I knocked on the door but no one answered. I knocked, no one answered. I groped over the lock with my old fingers. I wanted to die near my child, near her whom I loved. No one came.

"I rushed back home. I set the bellows going, melted and moulded. I filed out keys, as many as I remembered—it was many thousand; the night went on. I filed and filed; I had worked all my life, it was many thousand. I hung them on a string. I staggered out sinking under the burden. Now I remembered that she could not love me, I an old man who only had to die. I went back and got what I had saved up. It was more than I thought. If I gave her that, all I possessed, then perhaps she would let me die near her. Sinking under the burden, I staggered out.

"The wind caught hold of me; I rushed on. Exhausted, I arrived at her house. I groped for the lock; I tried the keys. One after the other, not one fitted. Not one fitted. It must have been a tiny part of the bit that wouldn't fit in; I knew it needed so little. I knew it. My heart stood still. I was shaking with the rain and the wind. I wanted to sink down. My life was ended, I wanted to sink down. Dazed, I staggered out into the street again, drifted about. It was empty and desolate; there was only me. I tried the keys in all the houses. I no longer asked for so much. I didn't ask to die near my child, near her whom I loved. I only asked for a human being, anyone, only someone that I could be with when I had to die. I tried and tried. I could get in nowhere. I sank down on the steps of a house I didn't know, and my heart struggled no more. They found me there in the morning with all my keys in my arms. The gold was gone. I hadn't been able to give it to anybody, they had only taken it from me. But the keys were still there; nobody wanted those."

He left off and sat mute.

Another said, "On the slope of a hill lies a very ancient village; it lies in the sun. The streets climb upward, upward. Their walls are whitewashed; the houses shine, just shine. I and my brothers lived there. They were happy and good, I was wicked and bad; there hadn't been enough to go round. They worked out in the fields. In the evenings they came home. I had a cramped forehead, I was without peace, I lay quiet in a corner and didn't speak. They sat and ate. I had such a grudge against them, I don't know why; afterwards they went out into the street and talked and sang. One played the zither. It sounded so lovely, I lay and wept. It was not a human being, it was a zither; its singing was so wonderfully lovely. They didn't say anything to me, they detested me. Why?

"I pined away. For me there was nothing. I got something on the quiet and put it in their food, so that they died. It was all I could do. It was all I had in life. It made no difference. All the houses still lay in the sun as before; everybody smiled and was happy. I pined away. I'm only saying this to ask why."

At that another said, "I hoarded joy. I stole it from others in order to have it myself. I wanted to be the happiest person there was. I never had enough. Things went well for me, I hoarded and hoarded, I was greedy for joy, I never got enough. I grabbed so much for myself that there was nothing left all around me and it was a big country.

"When I grew old I began to doubt whether I had been right in what I had done, whether with all that I possessed I could really call myself happy. I reproached myself about much of my life; I felt doubts about myself. But one day I met someone I had robbed. He tottered along, he was ill and wretched to look at. Then I realized that I was right. I was not like him. Then I realized my happiness, which I had stolen for myself. I was rich. He had nothing.

"A few days later he died. It was said that the last words he uttered were that he was better dead.

"I died, too, not long after. In the part where we lived I had enormous stretches of country where I went shooting in the autumn. One morning I went out to shoot alone although I was nearing eighty. It was raining; the woods smelled as they do in autumn. I happened to trip and the gun went off. The last I remember is that I wiped my mouth with the back of my hand. It was wet. I remember that smell of rain; that was the last. I remember it still and I am filled with all the happiness that comes from having lived."

So they went on with their stories.

Many of them never said anything; you wouldn't have known they were there. Among these was an old man, small and insignificant. He just sat there and listened to the others. He had a warm heart and took a lively interest in what each one of them said. But when he thought about his own life it seemed to him so humble and almost ridiculous that he was ashamed to think back over it. He listened when the others talked of their own affairs, and he lived himself through their lives; it was as though he had had none himself. Not but that he, too, had something of his own, something that was his and no one else's. He persuaded himself most of the time that what he called his own was simply that by which he lived the others' lives, that which enabled him to understand everything; himself he was nothing. But at times it broke through as something else. He could feel it so beautiful and strange deep down; but he wasn't able to give it to others.

He wanted to give. He wanted to open out. He too wanted to sit and talk of his own modest life, just as the others talked of theirs; of what it was like, what he thought of and what he felt while he lived. But just as he was going to bring it out, he was frightened at seeing how insignificant his existence must seem to everyone else. It must all seem so pitiable to them. They would have to laugh at him, make fun of him, and he didn't want that, because for him life was not pitiable or laughable, not even his own. So he only listened to the others; he had nothing to say himself.

In the others' existence life had been so much greater than in his. He saw that he ought not to push to the front with what he had, which was so much less. And thus everything seemed more beautiful, as great and beautiful as it really was. They had all experienced something great or rich; in them something had flowered and borne fruit. Perhaps they didn't always feel it themselves as anything so great; but he felt it, knew that it was so. So he listened to everyone and was happy in them. Those who spoke ill of life, he didn't believe those. But even in them there was such passion, such depth in their pain; he understood what their meaning had been and listened, as though to a vast river far away from him. For he had not experienced anything great himself, not felt anything rich and powerful within him. He had only lived with quiet gladness.

In a lavatory underground he had sat in the box and taken the money. For a penny he had given out a little paper; that was all. That was why he didn't want to talk about his life. It must seem to the others so meaningless and perhaps ridiculous. His whole existence had gone by down there. He had taken the job as a young man, not intending to stay; only so as to have something to do while he waited for his real calling. As time went on he had begun to see that this too was a calling, and that it was his. Why should he not be content? He filled a place that had to be filled; if he didn't do it, then someone else must. That being so, he could do it just as well. It was an insignificant place, but he was of no significance either. He was an ordinary man, and this was a place for an ordinary man. So he thought, and he stayed, and he was happy.

Although he sat down there from morning till night and seldom saw daylight, yet he came to understand life, and love it above everything. He understood that there was nothing ugly in it; everything was beautiful and good. Some parts were greater, some were less; but everything had its significance, nothing was indifferent or without value, nothing ought to be denied. Not everything could reach greatness. Some of it had to be strangely small, simply that the rest might be the more remarkable, might rise the higher; for life was rich, but not so rich as all that.

So he sat thinking down there, and as the years went by there was much he understood.

He learned to know humanity only as it came down

there to him. And yet he learned both to know it and to understand it. They made their way down there to him not to carry out any great deeds, not to live, not to be human in the highest sense; they came to carry out a common act which was shared by all that lived. But there was nothing low, nothing degrading to them in the act; they were something great and noble, and he loved them.

He particularly loved one kind of men, those who were strong, collected, those whom you felt life had taken hold of in order to use, in order to compel to its own end. There was such a calm about them, and even down here such a simple dignity, that they filled him with assurance and confidence. He could sit and hear their sounds from out of the closets; yet when they came out all memory of the act inside was blotted out for them. They were nothing but passion, nothing but a struggle to reach the one, the greatest. He was able to sit for a long while afterwards and feel glad about them, remember their faces, think how they were now going about up there in the sun and doing life's great deeds with a clear confidence. Such were his thoughts about humanity; that was how he saw it.

But humanity paid no attention to him, hardly noticed him. He handed them their paper; after that he meant no more to them. There were a few whom he recognized from a long time back. They came year after year, they grew bent and grey, they aged with him. But they didn't know him. Even now in eternity he still sat and listened for humanity and believed in it. They didn't know he was there; he might just as well not have been. But he was among them, and he was happy. Now as so often when he was alive, he sometimes longed to be able to give himself, to be able to open his heart, to make somebody a gift of what he had collected; but when he felt that what he possessed was not his, that with him more than with others it belonged solely to life itself, then he contented himself with listening, with gathering in and gathering in, as if he knew that it would nevertheless some time be passed on to another, to one greater than himself.

There were many less happy than he. Many were afflicted by their loneliness, by being different from everybody else; because no one was like them and so no one could feel the things they most deeply felt. There were two like this. They sat a little way off, by themselves. They could not understand the others nor be understood by them. They could not understand each other either, but they could talk together, each about himself. The one was without a thumb on his right hand. He had never had one, and it had made him lonely all his life. He had felt that he was something set apart, that he was different from everybody else; he felt it even now. He had not considered himself as an outcast, stricken by an unhappy fate; he had lived among men, met many, come close to many. And yet he had always felt that there was a certain something that divided him from them, an invisible wall which no one could penetrate or break down. They might talk to him as to others, they might think they had reached his innermost being; but they could not conceive who he was, for he was other than they.

Now as he sat in eternity he was able to see how right he had been in his feeling that he was something quite set apart, and to understand how deep his individuality lay in his nature; even now he was without a thumb on his right hand. Now he felt still more how perfectly alone he was. He could sit and listen to what the others said, but it would somehow glide past him. It was as if they spoke another language. He didn't understand them, and they didn't understand him, for they were not like him, without a thumb on their right hand. So he altogether abandoned himself to grief over his loneliness, dug himself into it, deeper and deeper, lived solely for it.

The other had all his fingers intact, but he had a black

spot on the nail of one middle finger. He had had it even as a child, but it had never been wiped out. He went through the whole of his life with that spot on his nail, he grew old, he died with it. The strange thing was that many did not even suspect his loneliness. They noticed nothing, and they thought he was like them. He was forced to smile gently when he thought about it: he was different from the whole world and the world had no suspicion of the difference. But he himself carried the spot like a burden that weighed him down to the earth. He sought mankind one after another, but no one was like him. He believed that the spot which made him a stranger in life would at last be wiped out by life itself, which gave it to him; but it was not wiped out. His loneliness grew and grew. It felt like an empty waste around him wherever he went. He didn't complain, nobody knew of his suffering, nobody knew that he sought and sought one in the whole world who was like him. He passed out of life without anybody suspecting his struggle.

Now that he sat here in the darkness he couldn't see the black spot on his nail. But he knew that it was there. He felt more deeply than ever the strangeness of his fate. There was an emptiness around him as boundless as the impenetrable darkness.

It was a quiet satisfaction to them both that they had found each other. They could sit talking together—after all, there was a little warmth in that—but they couldn't understand each other. They understood that they were both alone, but they didn't understand each other's loneliness. Each knew his own suffering, but he couldn't grasp the other's, only dimly sense it like a dwindling flame far off in the night. The one had a black spot on one nail, but he was not without a thumb on his right hand. The other was without a thumb on his right hand, but he had no spot on his nail. So their eternities passed.

Not far from them sat a man and woman talking in whispers to each other. They spoke so low that no one could hear what they said; you heard only the passion underneath the words. They had loved each other a whole lifetime. They sought each other still.

The man said, "When I love you it is as if I were living as a stranger far away in a great land where I was not born. I see the trees and the mountains; I see the clouds and the hovering birds, a great, strange land. I hear the wind rustling in the light woods; I hear the rivers roaring deep down in the valleys. And I stand listening and listening. It is not my land where I was born. When I love it I long for my own land far away, where I was born."

The woman said, "When I am with you I am happy."

But the man said, "You have never understood me. You have never reached me, nor I you."

The woman said, "I have loved you."

The man said, "You never understood why I lived. I have struggled and suffered, built up and pulled down. I have sought and sought, I have doubted and doubted. And you?"

The woman said, "I have believed."

He sat thinking about himself, saw everything, brought everything together. He said, "I have struggled in the cause of life."

The woman said, "I have lived."

They were quiet, each alone with what was theirs.

The man said, "Now we are both dead. And I still long for you."

The woman said, "And I am still with you, beloved."

But a simple working man who sat ignored among all the others then began to speak. He said timidly and as if looking in on himself, "I long for home.

"I had a little home in one of the poor suburbs, but we were not poor. We had two rooms and a kitchen, one with sun in the morning. Everywhere it was clean and cared for, with white cloths on the tables in the windows, and on the table in the front room a big yellow cloth that my wife had crocheted. We were happy and wanted for nothing. When I came home in the evening from the factory, where the work was heavy and laborious, I was black and sooty and I couldn't touch anything. I washed and changed my clothes. Until then I couldn't hold the youngster; but he wanted to come to his father as soon as I came in at the door. I had to keep him off.

"At first, before I had a home, I used to go to bed dirty, as I was. I didn't care. Nothing meant anything to me; it didn't matter. Now everything mattered. When I looked around me, every little thing meant that I was happy. We had supper together. Then we sat for a while; we didn't light the lamp. The boy came and climbed up onto my knee. He pretended that I was a horse and he was riding far away in a great forest where it was all dark, but the horse found the way home again. He went to sleep on my arm; the cheek that had been lying against me was red. That's why I long for home.

"Afterwards we sat and talked about him; it was as if we were talking about ourselves. My wife had a lilting voice which I can never forget. It began to get dark. I remember the pattern on the plates, and a picture on the wall. I remember the chest of drawers and the old brown sofa and the youngster's engine on the floor. That's why I long for home."

So he spoke, quietly, dreaming back to what had been his.

But in another part a man was talking about his life to some of them who found it interesting to listen to him. He was young. He seemed not to have needed very long for living. He described everything in great detail, from beginning to end; it seemed trustworthy and well thought out beforehand. Slowly he told his story.

"I arrive one evening at an old mill in the woods. It is not yet very late in the evening; it seems as if everything is fresh and beginning anew. The sun's light falls obliquely into the wood. The birds are still singing; it is like morning. The dew is on the grass; it wets my horse's hoofs. It is spring. There is a smell of earth and big trees.

"The road I am following seems to go through the miller's yard. So I ride in under the gateway, not intending to stay but to go on farther. But inside it is so charming and strange that I have to draw rein and look about me for a while. On all four sides run low white buildings, which look as if they have been whitened by the flour that has sifted out from the mill and from the sacks when they were loaded onto the wagons. Even the ground is dusted with flour. My horse shies at it and paws up the black earth with one hoof. But to me it seems altogether an idyllic scene. It is so peaceful with its sheltering walls, and yet there is some massiveness and richness about it that makes it impressive. In the yard stands an old cart, from whose front wheels the rims are gone and the spokes almost rotted away, until it looks as if it has gone down on its knees. It stands outside the mill itself, which is a massive building, broad and prosperous and with a big black hatch in the middle. As I sit there in the saddle, this hatch, which is a little way above the ground, is opened, and out of the darkness inside comes the miller and behind him his wife. I feel sure that it must be the miller and his wife. He is a powerful, swarthy man, with dusty clothes but with hands like an engineer's, oily, greasy, as if he tended an engine. He looks serious and dependable. But his wife, who would be about forty or fifty, is fat and jolly and looks like a great gorged beast which is waiting until it can manage to eat some more. Her breasts lie like fat loaves down the front of her body, which she turns full towards me, and two well-fed arms rest between them and her stomach. She looks at me with round good-natured eyes that haven't any brows, and greets me with a jerk of the fat neck. I reply in the elated tone of one who is on horseback and has ridden all day in the woods. The charming atmosphere of the place, too, has put me into high spirits. I tell them what a pleasant surprise it is to find such a secluded little corner here so far away in the woods; let them see how taken with it I am. The miller doesn't reply. He stands looking up into the air. But the woman gives me a soft ingratiating smile. 'Yes, it's lovely here.' I enlarge further on the excellences of the place, how spick-and-span everything is, how clean the curtains up at the windows are, how neat the yard is with its white flour, and how pleasing it looks with the old cart stuck there, the stumps of its legs in the ground. The miller's wife takes it all in. She stands straddled in the middle of the opening and beams. The miller stands with his legs together.

"At last she asks me if I won't come in and look around the mill. Yes, I should very much like to. So I jump down from my horse and look about for a ring in the wall where I can tie him up. But there are no rings. I shall have to make him fast to the old abandoned cart; that will be all right. Then I clamber up to the miller and his wife. It's a bit strenuous, for the opening is placed rather high up and there are no steps; my feet slip on the floury wall. When I finally get up to them I am panting from the effort. The miller's wife brushes me down with an amiability which seems almost familiar, and smiles so that two great tusks are visible at the very back of the otherwise toothless mouth. The miller is serious as the grave. We go on into the mill.

"The droning begins, but mellow—thick and mealy. The millstones don't make much noise, large and heavy though they are. They go around placidly; they put you in a lazy good humour. You feel there is a lot of flour between them; it is a rather agreeable feeling. The flour lies inch-deep on the floor; it shows deep footprints. The miller stands and gapes. I think how stupid he looks. But the woman beams; she's a friendly soul anyhow. She fusses around me, talking the whole time, and she seems now even fatter than before. I notice that there on her broad bottom is a narrow groove, just as if she had nothing on underneath. But I find nothing laughable in this. It seems almost repulsive to me. And yet I can't get it out of my mind. I follow her bobbing backside all the time, wondering how anybody can bear to go on like that.

"But now the miller opens a little door at the very back of the dim building, and a tremendous roar bursts in through the opening, and at the same time a violent draught makes the flour swirl around the woman and myself. I realize that it is the mill wheel and great masses of water falling, and I follow curiously after him. But the woman gets irritable and wants to know what he can be doing out there. He can't hear her for the roar. I turn my back on her and go out through the little door myself. I step onto a narrow plank which is wet and slimy; I am on the point of slipping, but I regain my balance and take still another couple of steps.

"Here it is really wonderful. I stand amazed and draw a deep breath. The enormous mill wheel with its slimy old paddles roars a vast and awful music, drawing it up out of the gloomy water down below. The roar is so powerful that I am half-stunned and have to hold onto a projecting balk that makes my hands wet and cold. It feels uncanny to stand like this, with the river sweeping past below you, black and menacing, and yet it is so vast, so immense, that it grips you. I breathe deeply with joy; draw in the fresh coolness of the evening looking down at the river which hurls itself on between steep and narrow banks. I remember now that I have heard the river in the distance during my journey through the woods and wondered why I never quite caught sight of it. I am glad now at having actually seen it; it drives violently against the banks, rushing and roaring, but it doesn't foam. It stays gloomily dark all the time.

"Finally I look around at the miller. He is lying crouched at the very end, greasing the mill wheel. It looks strange. His outstretched head with the black forelock over his forehead and the drooping moustache looks perfectly ludicrous in its infinite woefulness. The big fellow is talking to himself all the time; I can hear nothing, just see his mouth going. Things like that seem ridiculous out here where everything else is so imposing. I turn around again and stare down into the stream rushing past below me. Dusk is growing deeper and deeper. In the end the water gets pitch black.

"At length I walk back along the slippery plank into the house. I wonder what has become of the woman. She is still bustling about around the millstones inside, as fat and buxom as ever. When she catches sight of me she stops and smiles good-naturedly. But I can see that she is put out. She wants to know what we can have been doing out there so long. I reply that it was so magnificent that one could hardly bring oneself to come away, and ask her why she wouldn't go out, too. She says that it's so slippery on the planks, and besides she can't get through the narrow door. Then I look at her and burst out laughing; I can't help it. But she isn't uncomfortable. She strokes herself slowly over her fat thighs and gives me a glance whose meaning I don't quite understand. Then she wonders why her husband doesn't come, what he can be up to out there. He is greasing the wheel, I say offhand, as if that were perfectly natural. At that she goes to the door with an impatient jerk of her head. She sticks her head out into the darkness and calls to him. But he seems not to hear. She calls again; nobody comes. I go up to her to see what I can do. Over her head I can see him sitting there as before, doing the greasing. He seems so idiotic crouched there that I have to laugh. We both of us call out. But he neither hears nor sees. The mill wheel roars in the darkness, it is almost horrible; he greases and greases. We call out again, both at the same time. He doesn't stir. At that she slams the door so that the whole house resounds with it and fastens the latch on the inside.

"But immediately afterwards she is again amiability itself, just as if nothing has happened. And between her and myself nothing has happened. It is only her husband she is put out with, of course. We begin to talk about one thing and another, odds and ends, what fine weather it is, and how hard it may be to flay an elephant alive, the kind of thing you talk about when you don't know what to say. She shows a lively interest the whole time. In the end I say that I must be setting off, that I must be getting on farther and not lose any more time. She looks at me surprised and asks what I can be thinking of, what I mean, going on farther. Farther, I say; I mean I shall carry on a bit before it gets pitch dark. 'Carry on?' she says. 'But the road ends here!' 'What?' I exclaim, astonished. 'The road ends here?' She nods her head. She puts her arms on her stomach and a good-natured smile spreads over her whole face. Yes, this is the end, she repeats again.

"It is a bit of a shock to me. And here was I supposing it to be an ordinary road going on farther. 'No, sir,' she says, and smiles so that the two tusks are visible at the very back of her mouth, 'if you had wanted to go on farther, sir, then you should have turned off at the little fork, sir, a hundred miles back in the woods; there you should have turned to the left, sir. And then you should have gone to the right, sir, and then to the left, and then to the right, and then to the right again, and then to the left.' I exclaim, 'Good heavens!' She adds, 'That's the right way. But of course no one finds it.'

"I feel this really is a shock. But she consoles me good-naturedly. 'It's so lovely here, isn't it, so it doesn't matter. You can very well stay the night here, sir, and then try to begin again early tomorrow morning. I'm sure we shall make you comfortable, sir, as well as we can manage. And we've got an attic where you sleep like a log right on into the day.'

"I can't help feeling touched by her kindness, annoyed as I am at having been delayed in this way. I stand turning it over in my mind; then gratefully accept her invitation. It may really be a pleasant little experience to spend the night in such a charming and strange old mill in the middle of the woods; it will always be something to remember later on in life. And it really will be fine to have a bite of supper perhaps, and then stretch out in a good bed. I am glad things have turned out as they have.

"She leads me through a dark passageway into the dwelling house, and opens a door into a big comfortable room. She lights the candles, thick yellow candles that look to me as if they can never burn out; they spread a warm, cosy light over everything. She leaves me alone for a while, just getting something to eat, she says. There are clean curtains at all the windows, a freshly scrubbed floor, a big dazzling white cloth on the huge table. Everything is so wholesome and honest. I have to sit down and feel how well I am, how satisfied with everything. I'm hungry, too; it will be nice to have something to eat.

She comes in with the food. First, a great trough of porridge and a cask of beer, which she trundles in through the door with her foot. It is meal porridge with a thick layer of sugar and cinnamon on top, and a huge lump of butter in the middle and running down to the edges. We sit down one on each side of the table stuffing away till we choke, and drinking beer. We finish up the whole troughful. I gasp with the effort. She wipes her mouth contentedly.

"Next she brings in an enormous dish of fried eels floating in oil. They're so fat they quiver on the plate and slide away under your fork. We eat them with our fingers. The oil runs down our necks. They're very good. She eats a vast amount. I eat a good deal, too. It seems strange to me that I can eat so much; I don't need much as a rule. It's as if I'd never eaten in all my life. I drink beer with it till I'm fit to burst. When we have finally cleaned up the dish she goes out and gets the next course. It's the roast. It's so large that I can't see her as she brings it in; I feel I can't manage any more. But it is so deliciously browned that I have to try a little bit of this, too. She gives me a staggering helping. She helps herself to twice as much. We eat.

"We eat in silence. We don't say a word. I hear her chewing with the tusks at the back of her mouth, that is all. And I see her round eyes that haven't any brows. They are clear and natural; mine feel misted over, stupefied. I feel more and more bemused with the food and the beer. Most of all with the food, which lies so heavy in my stomach that I can't stir. I am completely befuddled. And yet I help myself to more. Seeing her eat, I can't bear not to eat as well. I eat dully, listlessly, force down the food bit by bit; at last the meat has almost come to an end. She shifts the last piece onto her plate.

"When she has finished she gets up with a motherly smile and goes out into the kitchen again. I feel as if my body were a lump of lead. I lean my arms on the table and gaze dully around me. I raise myself and let out wind so that the room gets as hot as a bake oven. I am drunk. But everything seems lovely to me. I feel thoroughly happy. Everything is so simple and natural and so different from what I had thought. I sit and ponder on life, and understand a great deal that I've never understood before. It fits itself together for me; it is all so calm and secure and healthy. I feel about everything that it is as it is. I am happy.

"She comes in with a fresh dish. It is pork, the boiled rump of a pig, fat as butter. It sticks far out over the edge of the dish. I look at it calmly. I find nothing strange in the idea of eating a little more. It no longer puts me off. I understand the meaning of everything.

"We sit down to it. I don't eat in the same way as before. I eat slowly, painstakingly. I eat in order to get satisfied. The food gives me pleasure, a simple, natural pleasure. I am completely sober.

"We don't speak a word. I think she looks a good sort. A real little countrywoman, as they ought to be. And she knows how to look after you. We eat. When there isn't quite so much left I make sure of helping myself to the rest; it's good to be eating. I sop up the fat with a bit of bread.

"Then for a sweet she brings in an almond cake, not so very large, I think. She cuts it into twenty slices. We help ourselves and eat in silence. I turn over a great many things in my mind. It is very good, this cake, with the sweet almond; it's satisfying too.

"When it is finished I get up from the table, push the chair under, bow to the woman and thank her. I thank her briefly but very courteously. It was both ample and good, I say. And taking a few unsteady steps round the cosy room and rubbing my hands satisfied and contented, I add, 'And now it will be fine to go and curl up for a bit.' 'Why, yes,' she answers at once, 'that will be fine.' And she throws me her motherly glance.

"So she takes a candle and tells me to follow her. We go through a narrow passage and up a poky staircase. I follow behind the whole time. On the stairs I see her backside and the groove. But I just see it; apart from that it doesn't bother me. I don't feel that it matters. We reach my bedroom. It is a cheerful, pleasant room with light walls, and three big windows looking out onto the river; I can hear it roaring down below. Against one of the inner walls stands a roomy bed with clean, freshly laundered sheets. The woman puts down the candle on a chair beside the bed; its light flickers over the floor. I get a great feeling of comfort and well-being when I look around me. It will really be fine to have my sleep out thoroughly. Seeing how contented I am the woman smiles with such a good-natured grin that the two tusks again stick out at the very back of her mouth; between them there is nothing but empty gums, which stand agape like a fox trap. She's admirable, I think. She arranges the bed a little, smoothes it down with a tender hand. Then she hugs her arms together under her breasts so that they lie there like lumps of dough in a great trough, and asks me if there's anything else I want. 'No thanks,' I reply, a little confused. So she goes towards the door. There she turns round and asks me once again, a little more sharply, it seems to me, if I'm sure there's nothing more I need. 'No thanks,' I say again, a little amused. At that she goes with a kindly good night.

"Once she is outside the door I begin slowly to take off my clothes. My body feels rather heavy and gorged. I take my time so as to enjoy thoroughly the prospect of going to bed. The candle flickers over the broad honest floor boards as I go padding about. Then I creep down in between the sheets.

"They are lovely and warm. Everything is lovely and warm. When I stretch out my legs they rub lightly against my knees, just pleasantly rough. It's lovely. I rest my hands on my stomach and gaze up at the ceiling. Everything is whitewashed and neat. Walls and ceiling. The tallow candle spreads its warm light over the room. White, clean curtains at the windows. And the river drones and roars down below. It's all very pleasant.

"I lie and ponder over life, how pleasant it is. I drowse off farther and farther and understand it all. I think of the woman. I can see her ripe and wholesome, so simple and straightforward. People ought to be like that; then you could really be fond of them. The food lies in my stomach heavy and good. I can't move. It's so lovely and warm all through my body, it gets better and better. There is neither beginning nor end to anything. My head swims a little. I feel slightly tipsy with well-being; it's lovely. I doze off. Then sleep, I suppose.

"Long afterwards, many years afterwards, so it seems, I feel as if somebody has come into the room. I half-open my eyes; it's the woman apparently. She has nothing on any more. Her fat thighs flop against each other as she comes up to the bed. But she is serious, not quite the same as before. 'You should remember to put out the light,' she says rather firmly; and she spits on it; it splutters. 'Yes,' I say, 'of course.' Then she creeps into bed.

"It seems just right to me. I am happy. I put my arms round her neck. With that she begins to open out to me. We talk about life. We feel the same about everything. She talks a lot about food. I do too. I tell her how much I admired her full figure from the very first. She lays the loaves against me. Then many years pass.

"I feel very drowsy and happy. I wonder for a moment how my horse can be getting on. 'He has eaten himself to death,' she says. 'That was a long while ago.' 'Oh, really,' I say. I think about life a great deal. I think how great and lovely it is. I love her a great deal; there is neither beginning nor end. And the miller? I wonder. 'He is greasing the wheel,' she says. 'Oh yes,' I say. Then many years pass.

"At last I wake; there is something droning a long way off. I sit up in the darkness, rub my eyes. I see nothing. But I hear something roaring and roaring, heavy and monotonous. It is the river. I lie down. It is the river. The woman snores. I hear everything. I am clear-headed and sober. She lies with her back against me; it is warm. The river roars and roars, stronger and stronger, more and more violent, undiminishing. It is all so tremendous it makes me dizzy; I can't bear it, it is too vast.

"I start up. I rush to the window. I throw it open. The roar bursts in upon me, furious, shattering; it seizes hold of me. I fling myself down.

"The water grips me; it is icy cold. It hurls me with it in its rush. It roars, roars. It hurls me against the mill wheel, against the great iron-covered paddles. They lacerate me; the blood foams, froths.

"But in the starlight I see the miller, waving his arms above his head, and shrieking madly with triumph and exultation in the darkness, his mouth wide open. It is boundless, overpowering. I give up my soul in ecstasy. Then there is nothing.

"Now that I am dead I don't know what it's about. I don't know what it meant or what it means. I only describe it as it seemed to me, nothing more."

He stopped.

Those who had been listening thought it a rather strange story. They made their comments, for it or against it. Then they too left off, returned to themselves.

But far away from them all, in another part, motionless and shut in on himself, sat a young man, dead long ago. His face was delicate and still kept its youth. He talked to himself every evening. He said, "She wanders down there among the flowers. She walks in the woods under the great trees and thinks about me. She sits outside her father's house and remembers me.

"It's evening now and she steals away on the noiseless path through the jungle and it grows dusk. She sits down by the river, on the low bank with the scent of the lotus flower. There she waits for me, while it grows dark. She waits for the white gleam of my boat with the water singing softly around it. She waits for the small singing waves and her lips smile in the dusk. She knows I am coming; she can smell the lotus flower at her feet. She knows I am coming, and her hands grow warm with the rapid beating of her heart. Now, while it grows dark.

"Beloved, this night I am not coming to you. This night I cannot come, not this night. But tomorrow I shall be with you. Tomorrow when it grows dusk my boat will glide up the river, through the singing waves. Tomorrow I shall be with you."

He left off. He stared yearningly into the darkness.

Then, as always, every evening, an old man by his side, with long snow-white hair, answered.

"Your beloved is dead. I sat and held her old hand in mine when she died. She was my mother.

"It must be more than a thousand years ago now, but I remember it all as if it were yesterday. My dear, gentle mother.

"She never spoke of you. But when she was gone I found a picture of you, faded after many years. That time when I first came here to sit by your side I recognized you from it.

"My mother was happy. My father was a good man. He took her when she was young, and she loved him with all her heart, for she realized that you were dead. She loved him all through a long and happy life. She has been dead a long time now. We are all dead now."

Then turning towards him with eyes burning softly, the young man said, "You say my beloved is dead. My beloved is not dead.

"It is evening and she sits by the river, on the low bank with the smell of the lotus flower. There she waits for me, and it grows dark. She waits for the singing waves, and her lips smile in the dusk. She knows I am coming; she knows I am close at hand.

"What do you know about love?"

The old man answered, "I am an old man. I lived so much longer than you, who died in your earliest youth. I know that love isn't everything. But life is everything. Yes, life is everything.

"Now we are all dead."

The young man said, "My whole life was love. My only deed was to love. Apart from that I have not lived.

"And if I could live once more my life would again be only this, to love. To love her whom I have loved and still love.

"I should seek her by the river. I should seek her in the dusk where she waits for me.

"What do you know of love?"

The old man answered, "I grew old. And I held her hand in mine when she died, my mother's small wrinkled hand.

"What is love, what is life, when we are all dead?"

Then the young man turned away from him, but spoke quietly into the darkness with an ardent voice.

"Beloved, this night I am not coming to you, this night I cannot come. But tomorrow I shall be with you. Tomorrow when it grows dusk my boat will glide up the river to you who wait for me where the lotus flower sheds its scent. Beloved, tomorrow I shall be with you."

So he spoke in the darkness.

No one answered him any more, the old man sat sunk in his thoughts, everything was empty and waste. But from far away, from far down in the darkness came a strangely drawn out, bellowing cry, infinitely plaintive, like a beast weeping. They all knew it, but they didn't know what it was. It was something that didn't belong with them.

It was a man who had lived too long ago. He sat on his haunches, he had hair over his body, his nose was flattened, his mouth huge and half-opened. No one knew who he was, not even himself. He didn't remember having lived. He only remembered a smell, a smell of a great forest, of resin and wet moss. And a smell of another being, of something which was warm like him, something which was like him. He didn't remember that it was a human being. He only remembered the smell. Then he sniffed around him in the darkness with nostrils distended and bellowed like a beast weeping. It sounded horrible. It was such an agonizing wail of boundless sorrow and yearning that they shuddered. But he wasn't one of them.

They lived their life, seeking and seeking, they suffered and struggled, believed and doubted; they didn't bellow.

No one spoke for a long while. It was desolate. It felt as if it were night around them and cold.

But for two children, a boy of twelve and a girl, who sat talking together without a pause, it was morning. For them it was always morning. They had so much to talk about that they neither heard nor saw anything else, and everything was fresh and certain for them. The boy especially could describe everything between heaven and earth; he stumbled over himself, he was so bursting with things to say. The girl admired him boundlessly. It was incredible how much he knew, how much he had met with and seen, how much he had found to do. And how thrilling it had been all the time. He snared pike in a lake in the summer, in a rushy creek. The sun blazed, the grasshoppers scraped with their thighs. It was so quiet that you hardly dared breathe, but there was a sucking when you lifted your feet, because it was soggy. He snared such a lot that he could hardly manage to carry them home. Then he fried them for himself and anyone else who was hungry; sometimes there was enough for a whole house, the one he lived in.

But he had a lot more to see to as well, although most of it had to do with the water. One Sunday, in the winter, he had had to pull out another boy who had gone through a hole in the ice before it was properly frozen. He was a good lad; it was well worth pulling him out. He was his best friend; he was sure to turn out well in time.

So he got to know about the whole world, and decided to be a sailor and see everything and do everything. And once in springtime he made himself a sailboat out of a plank and a shirt—one that he stole from his father, because he was bigger. He was going over to the other side. It was blowing just right; with the water grey, it made him tingle all over. But out in the middle came a wind that he had not reckoned with. It upset the plank and he was gone. But it was thrilling the whole time, and anyhow it was his own fault because he was clumsy with the sail. Yes, he had done any number of things, one sort and another.

The girl listened to him with shining eyes; she was as proud and enraptured as he was. She egged him on with delighted exclamations and little wondering remarks. She constantly wanted more. And there always was still more that he'd done. He had kept rabbits, and had his own potato plot which had to be looked after and turned over. He had gone in a train, twenty miles by himself. He could tell which clouds came with rain and which were only to look at. He knew when the sun rose. He had had a gun, too, and some days he would go shooting sparrows with it. That seemed rather cruel to her though. But when he said it wasn't, because anyhow there were so many left, then she realized that he was right about that. He knew the names of all the animals and was able to imitate their cries and all the other sounds down on the earth. He knew all about the world, an incredible amount.

She hadn't done very much herself. She'd only played hopscotch and picked flowers; she didn't know how to do anything else. But that didn't matter. Now she had him she'd got to know just the same what great fun everything was.

They were both happy. Things were all right for them, as they should be. And there was such a lot that there was no danger that they would ever get to the end. They realized there was enough. The darkness around them shone with things they had brought with them. They were perfectly happy.

A man said, "One morning, I went to put up fences for the animals who were to be turned out next day. It was early. I went through the birch meadows where I had played about as a child. They smelled of fresh leaves; and the secret places for wild strawberries, I knew them all. I went along thinking about nothing. I went thinking about the trees and the openings between them; I recognized them. I went along thinking of her whom I loved, who sat at home in the farm waiting for me and for our first child, whom she was soon to bring into the world. The birds were singing everywhere. The cuckoo was calling up on the hills where there were oaks. I thought about everything. I thought, I'll gather a few strawberries for them to eat at home tonight.

"Just as I was going along I heard something murmuring and muttering. It was the stream. I knew it well. I'd had a water wheel there when I was a boy. I went and walked a little way by the side of it. Some way up I found the stones that I'd jammed the axle in between; they lay just as they used to. There was a lot of water this year; good thing, the corn would be doing well. I thought of all the days in spring when I'd scrambled about on these stones. Then from farther down in the meadow I heard some youngsters playing and went along to them for a bit. They were busy with a water wheel which had tin on the edges of the paddles. It wasn't finished yet. They looked up, sweating. I said, 'There used to be a better flow farther up.' They said, 'It's stronger here now.' I looked on for a while. Then I went across the boggy patch up onto the path again.

"The sun struck warm already. I took some bark off a birch and made a basket, and gathered it full of strawberries; I knew the places. I didn't care so much for strawberries myself any more; it was for them at home. I came to our piece of land where my work was.

"I put down the basket in the grass. I pulled out the

fencing that I'd carted there the week before, and took some birch twigs for binding, for there wasn't much juniper on our land. The leaves smelled strong. I worked at my job while the sun mounted.

"I am thankful for a morning long ago."

So he talked of it; his face was fresh and clear.

One man sat thinking over what he had. He was a murderer. He had murdered a man, it had taken fifty years, he had had to learn. First there had been a long, long day, a brilliant unending day. He worked in the sunshine, his work was to lay foundations, the day had no end. He loved a woman, she loved him. They had many children. He took them about in the woods, he taught them about all the trees, about the sea and clouds and stones. They got bigger. The sons grew up, they thought his way. The girls thought their mother's way. They all grew and increased. He got a big beard. The sons were bearded, too, and spoke gruffly, like him. The girls were married and had children. The sons too. Everything increased, multiplied. There was more and more of everything. The sun shone and shone, it couldn't set. There was one whom he wanted to murder but it was too light. He worked and worked; he was always happy. The day never came to an end. He grew bald; he bought himself a fur cap. There was one whom he wanted to murder. Then it grew dark at last.

He crept out onto the road. Clouds were blowing across the sky. He crept across the fields. The other was in front of him the whole time. He stopped and listened, jumped a ditch, slipped into the wood. The branches crackled under him. He went on tiptoe. He crouched forward. He didn't breathe. The other was only a little ahead.

The ground took a plunge downwards. It became narrow, a narrow ravine. There was wind in the trees. Pitch dark. The darkness felt good; he unbuttoned his chest. The ravine got narrower and narrower; it plunged down. There were slippery stones and wet leaves in between. He dropped down and crawled. He crawled so as not to be heard. The other was almost within touch. He was crawling, too. He could hear him panting. He didn't breathe himself. He took a leap forward and got hold of him, hurled himself onto him. Then he stabbed himself.

He sat thinking. He sat here now, thinking. He sunk his head in his hand; then lifted it slowly and looked around him, questioning.

The hairy one bellowed from far beneath. He remembered nothing.

"I lived on a strange earth," said one of them. "It had fire in it. We lived on the soil and we were happy. We sowed and reaped, as our parents had done, like our fathers in all ages. We grew wine and corn in the big valleys; we planted the grey olive trees on the sloping hills. We understood the meaning of life. I will tell you what happened.

"There was a house by the hill. Giuditta lived there. Almost everything I am going to tell you is about her. She was not unlike the other girls at home, but she was more beautiful than them all. When she went along the road with her basket on her head the ground shone with gladness, and the swallows rose higher into the light, their wings at rest.

"There was always sun at home. There had been sun at home for as long as our people could remember. The sky was far off and high above us; at home there was nothing but earth.

"But Giuditta was more than all else. When she went through the village on her big bare feet she sang more cheerfully than the others. But in the evening when the girls sat chattering and laughing round the well she rested her head in her friend's lap and lay listening to them. Her breast was full and heavy. She smiled as if she were not yet happy.

"It was me she came to love. We loved each other like two children; we knew nothing about love. We sang and played together and in the evenings we climbed the old paths that ran steeply up the mountains where no one lived. We climbed so high that there were no more paths; then once we got lost. It had grown dark. Out of a cleft in the mountain came a feeble light. There lay a little house, of stone and mud, not like ours. We found our way there. We crouched in through the door. The house was cramped and low; you could hardly turn round in it. There was only one window, a square hole; it was set in one corner in the wall facing the valley. An old fire was flickering on the trodden earth floor. At first we couldn't make out anything. Then we saw an ancient creature, a hunched woman, sooty and lean. She sat poking the fire; she was one-eyed.

"'We have lost our way,' we said.

"'Yes,' she replied, as if she knew it.

"I could see that she was not one of our people. It was oppressive and strange. I wanted to get away from it, down to the valley again, to sun and trees, to houses and people. I knew I could get there alone once it was light again. But Giuditta sat down and stared like the old woman into the fire. She asked her who she was. The old woman said she was no one.

"'Then you are not human?'

"'No,' said the old woman, 'I keep watch over human beings.'

"Giuditta said, 'You shall read my future,' and she held out her hand. She lay close to the fire, her legs were red, her breasts were big and heavy. I knew how I loved her; I wanted to take her away, to rush through the darkness with her down to the valley, to houses and people, to sun and trees. I knew I could get there alone even in the dark; but she didn't hear me or see me.

"The old woman took her hand and looked at it a long while. Then she said, 'When you bear a child you must die.'

"Giuditta drew her hand away slowly. I stood pale. I could feel that I was trembling. In a strange, submissive voice Giuditta asked, 'Why must I die?'

"The old woman said, 'In you life has grown full.'

"We both went towards the door; neither saw the other. We stood staring down at the fire. We asked the way home. The old woman described it for us; it was easy to find when she said it. We went out into the dark. We went along silently side by side. We didn't hold each other's hand in the way we used to. I hadn't thought about life; I had only lived. I knew nothing of love. I listened for Giuditta's steps in the dark.

"The path plunged steeply. Giuditta stumbled over a stone. I put out my hand to steady her and touched her arm. I knew that I loved her and wanted to save her from all harm.

"We went farther and farther down the mountainside. It no longer dropped so steeply; we struck a path that I knew. Then it grew light. The whole valley was spread out broad and rich in front of us, the sun flooded it, it seemed endless. I breathed freely. I stood still for joy. I saw my father's house. I saw all the houses. I saw the trees and the birds, the whole of life. Then I thought I understood the meaning of everything, how great and light everything was.

"Giuditta stood close beside me. Like me she looked out over the valley. But her glance passed over everything veiled and withdrawn. Then she drew close to me and kissed me passionately with her arms heavy around my neck. I stood intoxicated; we had never kissed each other before. But when I looked down into her face I was frightened and held her away from me. I knew how I loved her, how I would protect her, cherish her, how I would live my life with her, live for ever. But then she struggled close to me with her whole body, tore her clothes away from her full breasts; they smelled milky. I breathed heavily, she bore me to the earth, gave up her body to me, I wanted only to live, only to live. She lay smiling. Her eyes grew dim and heavy. Life and death flowed together into eyes that saw nothing.

"We went on again in silence. We had not spoken to each other all the way home.

"My father's house was strange, strangely large and light. I built myself another, farther away. Giuditta joined me. We lived together happily. That year there was more wine than usual and more corn and more olives. I pruned the vine stocks bare so that next year they should yield an even richer harvest. I ploughed the fields black round our house. Giuditta was with child; she walked slowly along the meadows.

"Next spring came and she was to bear the child. It was a hot day, in the middle of the day. She didn't cry out, she only struggled. When she had borne the child she was dead. Her blood was too rich and fierce; it wanted her to die.

"I took the child in my arms. It was so small. I clutched it to my breast, looked around me, alone. The whole house was silent, only myself. I stood crushed with heavy pain.

"Then a long way off I heard a song. A monotonous, happy song that I recognized. I stood listening. With bent head I went outside the door, with the child held close to me.

"Through the valley came a slow procession. In front went a man carrying a symbol of the phallus on a pole. He carried it high in the sun. After him followed all the people singing. It was an old custom of our fathers for this day in the spring, in the time of fertilizing. I stood holding my child close to my breast; it was so small. I gazed and gazed as the great procession advanced. I thought it strange they should be keeping that feast today. The sun shone without end; they all sang the same monotonously happy song; I went to meet them across the fields.

"In the middle of the valley they stopped. I stopped a little way from them. I was like a stranger. I gazed and gazed at all the people. I saw my father, I saw my mother, I saw them all. And I saw all the trees and all the placid houses in the village, the whole of life.

"Then I thought I understood the meaning of everything. Then I understood that life wills only itself. It wills trees, it wills people, it wills flowers smelling on the earth; but not any one of them.

"Life has no love for you, tree; life has no love for you, man; for you, flower; for you, waving grass; except when it means just you. When it no longer means you, it loves you no more but blots you out.

"Then I understood the meaning of life.

"The sun shone. The sun shone as never before. It was charged with light and heat as never before. My head grew heavy. Dazed, I stood with my child in my arms—it was still wet from its mother's womb; dazed, I stood and joined in the happy, monotonous song, like my father and mother, like all people on the earth.

"Then the ground began to tremble under us. The mountains opened, burning earth burst out of them, poured down towards us, down over the valley, engulfing all; the sky shook with the roar.

"Terrorstruck, I pressed the child to my breast. But I stood motionless, just waiting. And when I looked round I saw all the people were standing motionless. They were just waiting. It was as though they understood that they must die. But they sang their happy, monotonous song, the only thing they had. We were consumed by the burning earth.

"Now all that is empty desert. Rocks that crumble, that turn to dust. Sand circling in the fierce sun."

He sat silent. Then he said quietly, "I don't think life wills trees and people; I don't think life wills flowers and waving grass, except when it means just that. Otherwise it would just as soon be nothing. Empty desert. Sand circling in barren space."

Then he stopped.

They sat oppressed at the end of his story. Many struggled with what was not theirs. But no one had anything to say.

Then at last a man spoke. He sat among the others, but it was not as if he were speaking to them. He was squatting, with his arms around his knees, motionless, but in his hand he held a staff like a wanderer.

"I am homesick for my country. I am homesick for the great desert where I was alone. I am homesick for my country which no foot has trodden, which no people has burdened with its roads. I am homesick for my country which has no bounds, for the burning sun which has no shade. For my sky which is waste and empty, which is red from the burning sand.

"I am homesick for my country where I wasted away and had to die. I am homesick for the great desert where I was alone."

They listened to him, wondering. They asked themselves who he was; they didn't know.

But now while they struggled in vain to overcome what had been said, another began to speak. His voice was slow and clear, and infinitely gentle. "I was the Saviour of mankind; my life was to suffer and die. My life was to teach mankind suffering and death, so to deliver them from the gladness of life.

"I was a stranger on earth. Everything was for me so strangely distant. The trees never came near me; the mountains lingered far off from me. When I stood by the sea its smell was as faint as a flower's; when I walked on the ground it could not feel my step. No wind touched me; my clothes were motionless, still. All is appearance, all is a waiting for what is. All is a longing for what is, all is pain at living.

"I called God my Father. I knew he was my Father and that heaven was my home, where he waited for me. I called distress my brother, because it delivered me from life and from what is not. I called death my best friend, who was to reunite me with him who for a few years of his eternity had allowed me to live. I bore the sorrow of all that lives.

"And mankind nailed me on my cross where I had to suffer and die.

"Then I spoke to my Father. To him I cried out all my humble faith and love. To him I cried out the anguish of living in all that lives, the yearning of all that lives home to what is. And he covered me in darkness, he covered the whole earth in darkness, in order to hide it from the eyes of the seeing.

"Then mankind bowed the knee around the cross. Then all mankind on the whole earth bowed the knee, and hailed me as their Saviour, him who delivered them from life and all that is not. It was empty and desolate the whole world over. I gave up my soul on the tree of the cross."

He ceased. Moved, they waited for his words. He said quietly, "When I came here, then I had no father. I was a man like you.

"And the sorrow of life was not my sorrow. The sorrow of life was a happy sorrow, not what I bore."

So he ended.

But scarcely had he ceased before another began to speak, in another voice.

"I was the Saviour of mankind. My whole life was sheer gladness. It smelled of earth.

"I did not come in order to save them; I saved them by coming. I taught them all the glory of life simply by living.

"I was born to rule over the whole earth. When I grew to youth I rode through my country. It was in the summer, the day was luminous. All was close to me, all men, all trees and flowers, all things on the ground, all was at one with me. Then I understood that life is all, there is nothing else. I took a woman, she bore me a son. He was like me; he, too, was for life. I gathered my people; I led them out to fight against others; I taught them all to live and die. We all fought in the sun, we the conquerors, we the conquered. We all saw the loveliness of life and how it had a beginning and an end. Heroes bled to death. The dead were forgotten for all the living.

"One morning, the war trumpets blew. I charged on my horse far in front of my people, without armour, but with gleaming weapons. A man thrust his sword into my breast. I drew it out and knew that I must die. Bloody, I went on fighting in order not to lose the last lovely hour of my life. I fought more mightily than ever in the brilliant sun. A youth came against me, arrogant as I. I struck him down. As he lay dying on the ground he turned and gazed after me with a long, strange look. It was not hatred in his gloomy eyes, but he gazed with envy after one who was going towards life while he had to leave all and die. I bared my breast and showed him my great open wound. He understood and died with a smile.

"But now when I felt death approaching I rode alone out of the battle and the clamour. With my bleeding wound I rode along over the lovely ground. I saw the flowers and the trees, I saw the hills and all the roads, I saw all the bright villages in the valleys, and the birds circling above them. All was so near me; all was at one with me. Then I understood that life was all, that there was nothing else. I died upright, gazing around me."

He ceased. Then he said, "And yet, nevertheless, it was not all.

"And the gladness of life was not my gladness. The gladness of life was obscure and incomprehensible, not like mine. I was a man like all others. I had perceived nothing."

When he had said this there was heard a young, singing voice, slender and timid, like a child's.

"I was the Saviour of mankind.

"I was born to tell them all, to reveal to them the innermost meaning of everything. Within me I carried the hidden nature of life, as others carry faith and doubt. When I thought about anything around me, I understood not only what I saw, but also all that I did not see. I came into a great room where everything was gathered together and where it was always light and still.

"Because it was light I stayed there a little while. I was just a child.

"I didn't think much about what I possessed. I only carried it with me. But I felt my secret growing within me. Each morning it was with me and there was sun upon the whole earth when I came out to play in the dewy grass under the trees. And I knew how everything stood waiting for me, how everything living stood waiting for me, everything happy and everything dejected, until some day I should utter what was mine, what, smiling, I possessed.

"I was only fourteen; then I had to die. I carried the hidden nature of life within me; therefore I had to die."

They listened dispiritedly to the childlike voice. They sat there silent and helpless in the dark.

But one declared, "As for me, I was head waiter at one of the biggest restaurants, known and frequented by all. It is a difficult and important position. It's a matter of understanding everybody's wishes and just what they want in order to have a pleasant time. I had an attractive personality and everyone regarded me as well fitted for my post. I knew how to arrange things so as to make it pleasant.

"It's such small things that count, but they take a lot of finding out. A few flowers in a bowl, tables tastefully set, that may make all the difference. And service without a hitch, that's more important than almost anything. It's not easy. You must learn to understand people's wants and adapt yourself to them. I knew all that, and they had confidence in me. When they left everyone declared that it had been very pleasant.

"I was indispensable. But I, too, had to go my way sometime, like everyone else. Then of course they had to find a new head waiter, for they can't get on without a head waiter. I hope he had an attractive personality so that they still have a pleasant time."

Shaken to their very depths they heard him to the end. Uncertainty and pain filled them as never before, harried them and took all peace from them. They didn't know where to turn with their thought, they wandered about with it, found peace for it nowhere.

At that a man got up among them.

It had never before happened in eternity that anyone had got up, that anyone had changed and become something different. They gazed at him, marvelling. His face was passionate as if it were burned with fire, his eyes flamed in the darkness. He didn't speak like the others. He spoke fiercely, his words coming vehemently one after the other.

"What is truth? Tell us, what is truth?

"This life that we live, it is only confusion, only riches without end. It is too much. It is too much, we cannot grasp it. We can only see the little that is our own, that which is too small. But all that is great is too great. We struggle and struggle each by himself, we seek and seek, but nobody finds anyone but himself. We sit alone in an endless space; our loneliness cries out in the darkness. We cannot be saved; there is too much of us. There is no way for us all to take.

"Then is life always just one of us? Is it never all of us, something so certain that we can all lean our heads against it and be happy? Is it never simple and one and the same? Is it never simple like an old mother who says the same words to her children every day, but feels her love deeper and deeper every time? Is it never a home where we can all come together simply as one? Is it so great that we can never grasp it? Never, never in eternity! Only brood and brood, each over what is his own, and see all the rest engulfed in a darkness where our minds can seize on nothing.

"I can't endure life's being so great! I cannot endure its having no bounds. I cannot endure my loneliness in a space which has no end.

"I will seek God; seek what is always true.

"We will seek God to call him to account for this bewildering life. We will all gather together, and set out and seek God, to gain certainty at last."

They listened to him intently. He had spoken in a way that held them all. He had touched something in them all, something which each one now knew had lain hidden within himself also, and which hurt as soon as anyone touched it. They had not felt the misfortune of life so deeply before; some had not felt it at all. Now at last they became conscious of everything. Now they all understood what helpless confusion life meant, how it was so much and so great that it gave peace to none of them, not even to the happy, not even to the richest, that for mankind it was without foundations, without solid ground to stand on, without truth. Now they understood how degrading it was for them to live as they did, without knowing, without really being able to believe. Now they understood to what desperate loneliness they were each of them doomed, surrounded by impenetrable darkness. And they understood that it must come to an end, that they must go seeking for something else, for something that was valid for them all, for light and certainty, for truth.

But some thought, is there really a God?

One said, "Is there really a God? I feel as if there isn't one for me." And another said, "I, too, feel as if there isn't any God for me." The passionate one answered, "One man cannot expect to have a God, but for us millions there must be one." When he had said this, they believed it and got up to follow him and call God to account for this incomprehensible life.

They found it hard to get up. They had made themselves comfortable each in his own way for all eternity; it had never occurred to them to make a change. They got up with great effort and at first staggered a little in the darkness. But when they had gathered around him who was to lead them they stood firm and close together, like a body of men in which there burns a holy fire. They felt that amid all the confusion and diversity there was at last something holding them together, their misfortune, their bottomless misery. They felt the depth of their despair, they felt how it united them, they made themselves drunk with it. They felt it as a vast power, as the vast power of man, which forced its way out of the depth of his struggling soul; they made themselves drunk with it. The happy could not conceive how they could have been happy. The unhappy regretted not having been more unhappy.

With the passionate one at their head they set off to call God to account for everything.

There were not many to begin with, not many by the standards of eternity. But on their way they gathered more and more, all the unnumbered who sat round about in the darkness. They came upon clumps of people who were deliberating one thing after another, one life after another;

they came upon those who were quite silent, so that they were not noticed until you were standing among them. They came upon the lonely who sat apart far off, cut off from everything. They gathered them all. They gathered happy and unhappy, rich and destitute, faithful and despairing, the strong and the weak, the submissive and the struggling, all who had lived. These all followed them. When it became clear to them what the great pilgrimage was for, that it was for salvation from life's dreadful confusion and from man's loneliness in his boundless space, then they all got up and silently joined the procession. The eyes of many burned with agitation and suffering; they united themselves in ecstasy with the others. Some drew themselves up slowly. In their faces there still shone the gleam of a secret joy; they joined the multitude gazing into the far distance. They all got up and followed.

At their head went the passionate one. He no longer spoke. He was only one of them, the one who led them on. But he carried his head high, he seemed a vast figure, fire lit up his features. In life he had been a shoemaker, sitting all the time; now he was gathering all the living to lead them to God. He had sat shut up in a little workshop that smelled of wax and leather. There he had suffered his own life; now he suffered the lives of all. They followed him as if he had been the misery they had known from the beginning of time. They saw themselves in him, their afflicted, shut-in soul, which when it got out of its prison found everything foreign and desolate and cold, which yearned for home again, but no longer had a home, since it was no longer imprisoned, but homeless among all that is. And they thought, as the endless pilgrimage drew out longer, and as more and more multitudes gathered from all parts of the darkness, of how horrible life was, how horribly great, even greater than they had ever suspected. And they thought of God, of him who had laid on them this unimaginable burden and who would now save them, give certainty and peace, of how mighty he was, how all-embracing; and yet there burned deep down in his great hungering soul a small flame that warmed him amid his joyless riches, as a flickering candle warms the wanderer's hands at the end of all his wanderings in the empty desert where there are no more paths. That he would give them.

The multitudes grew and grew. They became immense. They became so immense that no thought could grasp them any longer. They surged like oceans whose coasts no one sees and no one guesses at. They seemed at last to stand still, great surging seas which felt only how everything was flowing in upon them, everything lonely and struggling, everything confused and abandoned, everything seeking and seeking again, everything that had been. They were drunk with the sense that everything was being gathered and gathered to them, until outside there would no longer be anything. It took hundreds of years, it took thousands of years, it was all so vast.

Now the masses murmured as never before with all that was in them; they stirred and seethed powerfully, heavily; they broke against each other; they piled up; they flowed from one to the other, levelling themselves out; rose in other places, sank again. Then they became calmer and calmer. The outermost edge seemed to draw in a little, became fixed, no longer wavered, held firmly together like an iron band all that was within and received no more from the outside. Out there was only empty nothing.

But now at last when all that lived had been gathered together, and had mingled with itself, like waves that mingle with each other when a struggling sea grows quiet and motionless; then gradually something strange happened, something which none of them had suspected. When it had grown quiet quite, they were seized with the sense of being one, not more than one. They felt that they belonged together, one thing fitted to the other, everything fitted together, it was a whole. And the whole was so simple that they stood gazing around staggered and bewildered. It was not complex; it was only great. It was not great; there was only much of it.

Everyone discovered his own kind. It wasn't hard; it came of itself. After a little seeking everyone found where he fitted in, where he had fellows; it all fell into place. Life seemed to be only a few kinds, but incredibly much of each kind; and when these kinds had each sorted themselves out, they formed together only one kind, which meant just the same thing. The exceptionally unhappy found the others who had been exceptionally unhappy; those who really were happy found all the others who had really been happy; the believers found the believers, the doubters found the doubters, the struggling found the others who had struggled, the dreamers the others who had dreamed and yearned, the lovers those who had loved, the bitter scoffers those who had shut themselves up in bitter scoffing and contempt, the abandoned the others who had been abandoned, the magnanimous the magnanimous; and the bandits found the bandits, the great martyrs found the great martyrs, the heroes the heroes, the swindlers the swindlers, those who were nothing those who were nothing.

At first there was a murmuring confusion in these vast, surging masses, when everyone found his own home. Here swarmed hundreds of thousands who all looked just the same. You called to them, "Who are you?" They all replied with one voice, "We are Mr Pettersson, the grocer." Here swarmed an even more stupendous multitude. You shouted to them, "Who are you?" They all answered gloomily, "We are those who have a black spot on their nail."

But when all had established themselves in their own place, the masses fitted together with no boundaries between them, making only a boundless whole, and it gradually grew strange and quiet all around. Life didn't seem to be anything at all remarkable, only what it should be. Life seemed only to mean that they should all be and that they should fit together. It was a meaning so simple that there was nothing to be said about it, nothing.

There was no confusion. Everything was ordered and perfectly secure, exactly as it should be.

There was no loneliness; no one was so queer that there were not several millions just like him.

There was no point in any despair, any unrest and hopelessness; everything was in order. Everything was as it should be.

They stood bewildered. A deep satisfaction, a deep gladness and thankfulness filled them. They gazed around them with slow glances; everything was peaceful and quiet, everything was one. They thought of how they had distressed themselves, how they had fumbled and sought, how they had suffered and suffered, how they had tormented themselves with anxiety and doubt, how they had dug deeper and deeper into themselves and not found any bottom, how they had groped ahead in the darkness to find just one who was their brother, just one, just one; but it was too great and empty, all was too great, so vast that they could not grasp it. A deep gladness and satisfaction filled them now.

They were like a man who has struggled all night with the gale. When at last the morning comes and the sea suddenly lies motionless, without wind, and daylight spreads out over the endless quiet, at first, lit up with happiness, he feels that he has saved his life and that all is serenity and light, but then when his eyes have searched the endless sea again and again, he is gripped by the desolation of all that lies motionless around him and by the desolation in his heart, where there is no longer peril and darkness, only certainty and security. So with them. They were gradually gripped by the desolation in what they saw, in what they had found to be the certain and the true. All was so simple and uniform. All was so light and perfectly comprehensible. All was just as they longed and longed all their lives for it to be. They had nothing to struggle for, nothing to suffer. Nothing.

They stood disheartened. They stood irresolute and didn't know what to do with themselves, which way to turn. What had been theirs no longer existed. No anguish filled them, nothing. No unrest drove them on. All was complete and ended; all was as it should be. They no longer had any reason to seek out God. They understood it all themselves; there was hardly anything to understand. It was only what it was.

A dull silence spread over them; it was gloomy and empty.

Then a man got up among them and spoke to them all in a hoarse but piercing voice. He was small and doubled up, but he got bigger when he drew himself up; his face was fine and slender in shape, and when he spoke it quivered with a fierce inner glow. "What then am I! What then am I!

"This life which we struggle in and suffer, which weighs upon us like a darkness where we are lost, which we feel our way through by anxious thought, groping and groping ahead to find at last what the truth is for each of us, this then is nothing but an unchanging repetition through the ages. It is nothing but the same over and over again, nothing but one and the same continuously; the same poor, simple meaning, the same certainty, the same nothing. We struggle and struggle; and then it is nothing. We tear open our breast; and then there is nothing but a heart which will live and die, like thousands more before it, after it. We feel a holy fire burning within us great and mighty; and then it is only the fire that's required to keep us going, the warmth of our bed to save us from freezing, poor wretches, and come to an end.

"So that's the reason for it all, only that we should not come to an end. That we should never come to an end, never come to an end. And when our evening is drawing in, we are brought back like great fat cows, who have each grazed its own bit of the sunny earth, and are driven together, each into its stall; and all that we leave behind us is the manure for next year's grass, our manure, as good from the one as from the other.

"I am weighed down to the earth with shame. I rise up in disgust and hatred. This life which is only an imposture, which is one long insult to all that I have felt holiest within me! This life which is so simple and small that it is humiliating to live!

"No confusion, no sorrow. No misery, no bleeding wound. No quivering heart which never finds peace. Nothing. Everything that for us gave life its richness and pain, which filled us with anxiety and groping unrest, with yearning without end, that is nothing. All that is is something other than myself.

"I was one alone, I was one in despair who never found peace. I was one without a home who went on seeking and never found. What am I now? Nothing. I am alone no more, I am nothing. No one is alone by himself, no one sets out alone on a road which has never been taken before, which is blotted out behind him. No one is alone with his heart bleeding to death, growing silent in a darkness where no one listens.

"I am not alone, I never shall be again. All is empty, all is in vain.

"If a man moves his hand out to the right, then slowly to his breast where he draws a cross, then up sideways into the air—that means nothing; then puts his finger to his lips, as if sealing them, draws an invisible circle above his head, and after that raises his finger and points towards a hidden star far off in space, which he cannot see, only feels is there; yet tens of thousands have done the same before him, even if only, as I now, in order to be alone in something amid life's emptiness and nothingness. It is horrible.

"It is horrible. I rise up in flaming hate. I rise up burning with hate against him who insults my holiest possession. I seek God! We will seek out God to call him to account for the poverty of life. We will seek God to accuse him of life's insult to man, of its certainty, its one poor truth. We will seek God to demand of him the confusion and the doubt, the soul's longing that nothing can still, to demand of him his boundlessness, his anguish, his space without end."

They listened to him with rising excitement. His hatred infected them. They felt that within them, too, it lay fermenting; within them all it grew stronger and stronger, it surged out over the illimitable multitudes, passed on by each of them. They saw his fine, quivering face. It was their face, a prayer for pain and throbbing unrest, for the soul's loneliness that nothing can redeem. They understood the brutality of life, its brutal gladness that wanted to rob them of everything.

All around they began to cry, "We will seek God." Farther and farther away they began to cry, "We will seek God to call him to account for the certainty and serenity of life, to demand of him all the anguish, all the darkness, all the depths of the abyss, all that we cannot grasp." Then thousand-voiced, as if from vast struggling seas, there rose a great roar, "We will seek God to call him to account for everything."

Slowly they began to move, the spiritual man at their head, leading them.

It was a strange journey. The immense multitudes, now greater than ever, rolled forward, spending all their strength. They rolled on so slowly and heavily that their emotion grew deeper and deeper. Their souls were filled with a glowing, mystic faith in the greatness of what they were undertaking. They went on and on; they did not arrive. They went on and on, hundreds of years, thousands of years; they did not arrive. Then they thought how tremendous this was that they were doing. They thought how incredibly vast they were, how incredibly vast was their poverty, rolling away towards him who possessed everything. They thought of God, how he lay jealously brooding over his treasures, cruel, demoniac, leaving for the swarming life which he had created only a tiny scrap of his incomprehensible nature, a poor morsel of bread, a little gladness and peace, a little certainty and warmth-giving sun. They thought with mingled horror and exultant vengefulness how they would soon stand face to face with him.

They did not arrive. The way to God seemed infinitely long. The spiritual man himself could not find it. All the noblest had to come to the front in order to try together to find the right way. They were dignified and serious men, but now, roused in their innermost being, they advanced with tightshut mouths which betrayed nothing, though their faces were flushed, overwrought. They scanned and scanned the darkness around them. Behind them followed all the others, patiently waiting and waiting, sometimes stretching up to try to look over and ahead of them, then again merely following them, going on and on. All around them was nothing but desolation and emptiness. They did not arrive.

Then at last they saw far off a feeble light. It shone steadily, but so feebly that it could scarcely be distinguished amid all the darkness. They made for it. They thought, it is a sea of light, but far away from us. In the end, after many years more, they began to approach it.

It was a little lantern with dusty glasses, casting a quiet light around it. Under it stood an old man sawing wood. They could see that it was God.

He was bent and short, but strongly built. His hands were rough like those of a man who has worked all his life long at one and the same thing and without resting. His face was furrowed, full of toil and a mild seriousness. He didn't notice them.

They came to a halt.

They stopped, struck with amazement before him. They stared and stared at him and could take nothing in. Those who were far off stood on tiptoe so that they, too, could see. A murmur went from man to man, a duller and duller murmur.

Right in front stood all the noblest of them, men with spiritual features, faces quivering with the soul's most secret life. Their eyes blazed with holy indignation.

"You are God?" they began in a trembling voice. "It is you who are God!"

The old man looked up at them, confused. He made no reply, but moved his head in assent.

"You stand there sawing wood," they said.

He made no reply. He wiped his mouth with the back of his rough hand, looking about him timidly.

"We are the living," they said. "We are the life which you have brought forth. We are all the living, who have struggled and struggled, who have suffered and suffered, who have doubted and believed, who have groped on through the darkness where nobody can find his way, who have sought and sought, known glimpses and yearning, who have reached out searching to the farthest point of our nature's uttermost limits, who have torn the heart out of our breast and cast it beyond the limit, to bleed to death in the nameless pains of loneliness.

"What have you meant by us?"

The old man stood perplexed and troubled. It was as if he had only now fully understood what it was about and who they were. He raised the frightened eyes of a recluse and gazed out over the surging sea of men who stood before him. His glance strayed about; there was no end to them. Wherever he might look, there was no end. It was illimitable, man by man, millions and millions again; there was no end.

He returned to himself. He stood timid and awkward, not looking up. He put the saw aside. His clothes were old and worn; it was more noticeable now. He passed his hand through his lank, grey hair, let his arm sink again. When he didn't have his work it was as if he didn't know what to do with his hands.

"I am a simple man," he began at last in a submissive voice.

"We can see that," said the leaders. "Yes, we can see that," said all the others, all the millions of millions, as far away as you could imagine them.

The old man got even more confused. He stood before them humble, weighed down by their words.

"I didn't intend life as anything remarkable," he went on submissively as before.

A shudder passed through the leaders.

"Nothing remarkable! Nothing remarkable!" they burst out, their eyes blazing. "It's horrible."

"Nothing remarkable!" sounded from the millions of millions. "Listen, listen to that! Nothing remarkable. It's horrible. Horrible."

The old man seemed overwhelmed by them. He fumbled with his large hands. His old head was bent still more. You could see how he suffered and struggled. At last he seemed to collect himself, withdrawing completely into himself.

"I have done the best I could," he said quietly.

There was something touching in his simple answer, in his inability to stand up against them. The leaders felt it, but they went on speaking just as sternly and severely.

"You have hurled us down into pain and torment, you have hurled us down into anguish and agonizing unrest, into nameless abysses; you have let us suffer and suffer, you have let us sink under our burden, under our misery, dragging us on. You have vouchsafed us the intimation that in suffering our life became great and precious, precious to eternity and God. You have let us languish, despair, perish. Why, why?"

The old man answered quietly, "I have done the best I could."

They went on.

"You have given us sun and gladness, you have let us be drunk with the loveliness of life, with the loveliness of morning when the dew wets our feet and all the trees smell and all the flowers and all the hills; you have let us know the earth's happiness, that our home was there, that our home was the flowering earth; you have vouchsafed us the intimation that life was gladness only, only radiant light, only morning and morning again. Why, why?"

He answered quietly, "I have done the best I could."

They went on.

"You have not believed in the one, nor in the other. You have just seen that in this way it would fit together, that in this way it would work. All you have wanted is that life should manage to keep going, and that it never need come to an end. All you have wanted is life, nothing more, only life over and over again to no purpose. Why, why?"

He answered quietly, "I have done the best I could."

At this unchanging answer they were at a loss. Something submissive and touching in it, repeated like that by the old man, made them stand silent for a while and collect themselves before they could go on. But soon their passion burst forth again, strong, irresistible.

"But what did you mean by it all then? You must have meant something. What did you intend by this that you set going, by all this unimaginable life? We must demand a complete understanding of everything, and also the confusion which is in everything. We must demand certainty about our radiant joy, about our right to light and happiness; and also the certainty that there is no joy.

We must demand the deepest abysses of anguish, our suffering which nobody can grasp, our anguish; our darkness where we languish and die, and also the certainty that there is no cause for anguish. We must demand coherence in everything, peace for our thought, for our tormented, struggling heart, and also we must demand that there shall be no coherence, no rest, no peace. We must demand everything."

The old man listened to them calmer than before. Outwardly he was not changed, and yet he seemed different, though just as humble as before.

"I am a simple man," he said, looking at them. "I have worked untiringly. I have stood by my work day after day for as long as I know. I have demanded nothing. Neither joy nor sorrow, neither faith nor doubt, nothing.

"I only intended that you need never be content with nothing."

This sent a stab through the hearts of all the leaders. They met his calm glance, so unlike their own ardour. They looked at him and he seemed to them to grow; he became great, so great that they could scarcely grasp him any longer, and yet he was so near to them. They grew quite silent; something warm rose within them, something unknown and new; their eyes became moist, they couldn't speak.

But all the millions of millions, all those who stood behind them and who had not been able to catch the old man's words, among them the unrest continued as violent as before, even more violent. They somehow gathered that the old man was being stubborn, wouldn't come out with the truth, and all their bitterness welled up. They must get their way with the obstinate old man. But they noticed that the leaders no longer spoke for them. They had given up the struggle; they had abandoned them. They didn't care about their salvation, their distress. They would have to fight out the whole struggle for themselves, although they had no other weapon than their bleeding breast.

Among them there stood an immense crowd of little children who had been playing and passing away the time as well as they could during the long journey, which they didn't know the meaning of. These they chose to plead the cause of this horrible life. These they brought up before God. And they all cried bitterly and sternly, "What did you intend by these, then? What did you intend by these innocent children?"

The children at first stood ill at ease looking around them. They didn't know what they had to do; they didn't understand what they'd been told. They stood uncertain and looked at each other. Then they gathered around the old man. Two of the smallest went up to him and stretched out their arms; he sat down, they climbed up on to his knees. They looked into his big horny hand, they poked with their small forefingers in his beard, on his old mouth. They thought he was a nice old uncle and pressed against him so that he should put his arm round them.

Big tears welled up in the old man's eyes. He stroked their heads with careful, stiff fingers that trembled.

"By them I meant nothing," he said so quietly that they could all hear. "I was only happy then."

Everyone's eyes filled with tears. They stood looking at God with all the children around him; every breast grew warm and full. The men tried to keep back what they felt; the women sobbed aloud. Every mother among the unnumbered multitude saw that it was her child who was sitting on God's knee, whose head he patted, and she wept, but subdued, softly, from joy. It was quite quiet; only the weeping could be heard. They all stood and felt deeply and secretly their intimate oneness with God. They realized that he was like them, only deeper and more than they. They did not quite understand, only felt it all. A miracle had come upon them. They all felt who he was;

the noble after he had spoken, the people of simple feeling, who couldn't afford to be noble, after what had happened with the children.

No one spoke any more. They had nothing they could say; and they were silent not from sadness, but because their hearts were too full. They were silent that they might feel and grasp everything. They were silent that there might be complete stillness. They went out of themselves in order to be with what had happened to them.

Gradually the weeping ceased. Gentleness and peace came over them, as it does after a shower in summer, when the earth lies damp in the sun, clearer and as if nearer than before. And they understood that their visit to God was fulfilled.

Yet for a while they remained, lingering with what had happened. Then at last they turned around in silence, beginning the journey back. Once more they looked towards the old man, who remained there; then they raised their eyes to the darkness before them.

The children didn't want to part from God, they liked being with him. But he patted them on the cheek and told them to go with mother and father and trust them, and they did as he told them. He stood alone gazing after them, serious and happy. And he vanished from their sight; the feeble light was hidden away in the darkness.

Mankind went on and on once more. But the vast seas no longer surged in unrest; they had found peace. The hosts advanced slowly through the darkness. All hands were raised, all eyes open. Silent and thoughtful they advanced. What they had experienced with God was gathered together and fell into place for them. The secret was mingled with the manifest; then the secret sank down to the depths of their soul while what was manifest was spread transparent above it. Each thought of what was his; each one was alone with himself. But while they were thinking they felt their oneness with all the others; while they were by themselves they felt they were all among the others. Slowly and imperceptibly as they advanced together there collected within them, as if in different vessels, something that was the same for all. And they carried it proudly or humbly; they carried it in vessels of a noble form which made the bearers noble as well, or in one of those country pots of clay in which the peasant women fetch water from up in the hills, when the wells down in the villages have dried up in summer. They carried their wealth; it was the same for all. They were all slowly filled with the same perfect inner certainty, faith and light.

Then they began to speak, each of what was his, but turning to the others that they might hear and believe. They spoke to each other as brothers, simply and quietly, one by one as something ripened and came to certainty within him. They spoke to each other as before, only more quietly than before. They no longer had so many words nor so great; they didn't give the whole of their inner selves, they gave only their faith, that which belonged to all. This they offered each other with opened hands.

There walked an old man. His head was aged, but he looked straight ahead, as if a long way still remained for him. He said, "I acknowledge you, dear life, as the one thing conceivable among all that is inconceivable."

And he walked among the others, holding silence, listening.

And century was added to century, millennium to millennium, age to age; they knew nothing of that. They only walked ahead, side by side.

Another said, far off from him, "I allow that life can be good and evil; I thank it for everything. I thank it for darkness and light, for doubt and belief, for evening and morning. In me it is the one; in my brothers everything else."

Another, who had lived shut up in himself, but now walked in freedom as one among them all, said, and he found in this his strength and peace, "Any real life is disheartening because it gives only itself, because its limit is fixed and closed, because the clearer its limit the more it suggests what lies beyond and the immensity of it.

"And yet I know, now that I have found peace, that only within narrow limits can man experience what is greatest."

Another said, "I am grateful for my unrest, which has given me peace. I am grateful for my anguish, which has shown me it is not myself.

"The sea at rest need not hear the gale to know that it is vast and deep."

So they talked among themselves.

But one said, "The shepherd watched his flock up on the hill, while inside it began to bubble and boil with lava and destructive forces. He knew nothing of what was happening there, and so he was calm. He drove on the flock in the sun and rested with his staff on the ground while he looked about him.

"Then in spite of everything when the catastrophe occurred he somehow understood that, too. He spread out his arms in the air and shouted at the top of his voice like a madman. That, too, he had within him.

"Neither the one nor the other was wholly himself. But when later on he watched new flocks on new hills, which he knew just as little about, he rested his staff on the ground with a new sense of security while he looked around him in the sun and smiled."

They listened to him and felt the same as he, only a thousandfold; it was something they all possessed in common.

And after a while another one among them began to speak. There was something fine in his voice, something humble.

"Perhaps there is something other than us; perhaps there is something other than living. But of that I know nothing. It is not me. We sense everything but we exist in what is ourselves."

And one of them said, "If our existence had no basis, we ourselves would have to lay the foundations of it. Fools and madmen would say that we were building on empty nothing. We men would only build and have faith. And the foundations would rest immovably on what we had built upon. For there is no nothing."

So they talked among themselves.

And they thought of God, of how he stood over there by the eternal light of his little lantern; and they were filled with security. They went on into the darkness. Behind them followed all the little children, chattering and laughing, running around each other. They had invented new games to make the time go quickly, and now they played them together, while the grown-ups thought about everything.

Another said, "The wealth of life is boundless. The wealth of life is as great as we can grasp. Can we ask for more? When nevertheless we do ask for more, then all the incomprehensible exists as well, all that we cannot grasp. As soon as we are able to reach out our hands for something, as soon as we get the feeling that something is, immediately it is. Can we ask for more?"

They were filled with gladness at these words. They walked in silence, all the gladness and wealth within them. They went on and on in the darkness without speaking, strong and free.

At last, humbly and quietly, one of them said, "It is mankind's duty to be happy."

And these words seemed to them to carry the whole of their faith. Simple as they were, they moved them deeply. They advanced in silence, thinking, with a secret light in their faces.

But one of them said, "We are not happy in the way the poor and miserable ask to be. We are happy in the way that man is happy when he is occupied with living his life."

And again another:

"One must take pains seriously over joy. A man should bury his grief in an ocean of light; and everyone will see that all the light is streaming from this one little grief, as if from a luminous gem, wrenched with toil out of the dark mountains."

So they thought, seriously, about their happiness.

But one whose voice was much more radiant than theirs then spoke.

"A man who bore an almost crushing sorrow, and who struggled heroically with life but came near to being defeated by it, saw as he passed a house on the road a two-year-old child sitting in the sand and playing with a dog. The dog was only a puppy and waddled clumsily about on its big paws. It pushed its wrinkled muzzle into the child's back; he shrieked with delight each time, clapping his small hands in rapture. He sat waiting without looking around, and when the dog nudged him again his eyes shone in the sunlight. A little way off stood a young woman looking on, as happy as the child.

"The man had to stop and smile; it looked so funny. But he smiled for their sake too, so that they should know that he thought they were happy. Then he continued on his way. What had happened had no connection with his struggle and his life, and he forgot it. But without his knowing it the trivial interruption still lingered within him, and when he gave himself up again to his sorrow and went on thinking out his bitter struggle, he was smiling even while he thought."

Another said next, "It is a fact that a hunchback is born into the world every minute. It seems, therefore, that there exists in the race a definite need to be in part hunchbacked. At the time when I lived there were some who discovered this, and they understood through it the whole abysmal cruelty and misery of life, and they preached a deep despair to mankind as the one truth and greatness, the one salvation, the one thing that could raise them to something higher and nobler and bring them a bitter peace. Nevertheless, however fervently they taught their faith, there were none the more hunchbacks born into the world for that, only one a minute as before. And in despair even over that, they had at last to give up and try instead to be happy."

So they talked among themselves. Each found in the depths of his soul something to offer, something of light and goodness. And they listened to each other, together building up their faith.

The millions went on and on. They advanced, vast, unimaginable in the darkness; but no darkness existed for them. They began to approach the place where they had first gathered together and where now they must separate again. The time for leave-taking came upon them.

Then while the others kept silent the aged man again raised his whitened head and said, looking before him as if a long way still remained for him, "I acknowledge you, dear life, as the one thing conceivable among all that is inconceivable."

After that no one said any more. What needed saying seemed to them to be said. Nothing was left but all the richness in them which their thought could not embrace; they hid it secretly within themselves. Without speaking they parted from each other to return each to his own place and go on living.

Guest of Reality

IN a small Swedish town there was, as everywhere, a railway restaurant just by the station. It was so near the line that smoke from the engines drifted across it and left soot on the front. The house would have been white otherwise. It seemed almost to have been meant for a sort of dream castle, a fairy palace; there were turrets and battlements everywhere, little balconies that you couldn't come out on, ornamentation and carving all over it, niches that should have held urns with flowers, any number of bare flagpoles on the roofs. But after all, it was no more than a big desolate-looking house with soot on it from the smoke. Yet it was not deserted. You could even see something of a festive air about it. Travellers went there for a glass of beer, had a meal there between trains, and in the evening the band played in the garden at the back. It was a castle that had been put to other uses or got shabby because the festival went on all the time, had neither beginning nor end and no climax. The linoleum in the dining room was worn, the plush sofas were fallen in and shiny with all the people who'd sat on them, the floor in the third-class refreshment room was worn into hollows with knots sticking up, the chairs were rickety and there were holes in the seats. It didn't much matter; it wasn't worth worrying about. The customers came just the same and in any case they'd have had to go away again immediately. They were no guests in a festive castle, but still they sat there for a while eating and drinking, while the trains waited for them, shunting up and down the line, until the bell on the platform rang and they went off.

There was never any peace; it was always people in a hurry who had to get away. But the castle stayed there the whole time with all its turrets and battlements, its flagpoles and balconies, its empty niches, always just as queer and fairy like, always drawing people to it as if to celebrations.

On the upper floor of the house they had fitted up a flat where a family with many children was living. Perhaps they'd meant to put hotel rooms there, where travellers could stay the night—there'd have been room for several off the long dark corridor—but nothing had come of it and they'd only made two rooms and a kitchen, where the family had lived for many years. At first, when they came there newly married, the flat had been altogether too big, but then the children had been born and grown up, more and more of them, and so it had got too small. But they never thought about that. This was their home and you didn't shift things like that, to their way of thinking. The rooms were small and didn't get enough light. The three narrow little windows that they each had were set high up under the roof; it had been done for the sake of the outside, so as to make it look quaint. The furniture was old and hadn't much finish. You could see it hadn't been bought in the town. The marks left by the strokes of the plane could be felt under the brown paint of the big bed and on the settles where the children slept, the sort that pulled out wider at night and took up a good part of the floor. In the best room there was a big round table with a crocheted cloth. They ate there on Sundays; at other times in the kitchen. On one wall hung a picture representing Luther; on another an alphabet embroidered on canvas with a lot of flourishes and ornamentation in a glass frame. Above the chiffonier was a little shelf with an old worn Bible on it, Arndt's *Homilies* and two new Bibles which the biggest girls had had when they were confirmed. They were covered in writing paper, fixed with sealing wax inside. That's more or less how things were. Many-coloured home-made rag mats covered almost the whole of the floors so that it was quiet when you walked. It was nearly always quiet there, although there were so many of them.

Under the windows there was a ledge, and there the smallest children went. They sat hunched up like young birds and looked out. They each had a stool. It wasn't really his own; it had been passed on almost like a legacy from the older ones. They didn't need it any more. All children have stools, you always find that. But these children had them so that they could sit up at the windows and look out. The trains were constantly going up and down, shunting on to different lines; the engines whistled, pushed the trucks off into the siding, the men ran along by the side and waved their arms. There was always plenty to look at. Sometimes when the wind was that way the smoke drifted across the windows, and if they were open you had to hurry up and shut them. Then you could tell how quiet it really was indoors; the noise outside only sounded like something a long way off. Still you could see it all just the same, the trains drawn up at the platform and then going off and disappearing, with the white plate on the last carriage, the engines shunting backwards and forwards just the same. On the window sills there was a thin layer of soot that Mother wiped off, but it kept coming

You don't often find such quiet in the world as there was in this home. The father was home for meals and he used to come in for a little while between times if he could. He was on the railway; that was why he lived here. But the mother was there all the time seeing to everything that had to be done in the house. That kept her busy. There was always something to be done and she seldom got out. She was fair, with clear grey-blue eyes, and her thin hair parted on her forehead. People are fair in many ways, but she was one of those where it isn't just an outward matter but you feel that it's for the sake of this very thing that the people themselves are; that they're able to be and live for it and nothing else would have been any good to them or given them enough support. People like that often seem fragile, as if it wouldn't take much to wipe them out. If a powerful hand brushed over the world a bit too roughly, they would be wiped out, would no longer be there. And the world would wake up as if out of a good, pleasant dream and realize that everything was just the hardest reality. But these very people have a strange certainty and security. They go about quite unperturbed, not like pale shadows but as if they were completely real. It's as though they were certain that they won't be wiped out, that they'll be there for ever and no harm will come to them. They seem to belong to an old race that has lived in every age, from the very first. Although everything may have changed and been laid waste, they have always been saved from harm, they who were the very easiest to break. They have been and will be as long as life endures. And the world will never really wake up out of its dream.

She was one of those. She was nothing unusual or remarkable, went about the kitchen and the rooms doing her everyday jobs, chatted to the children, washed up after meals, did the washing and ironing, nothing out of the ordinary. When she had nothing to do she darned stockings, mended clothes. Going about her jobs she was nearly always cheerful and used to like it if the big children had a joke about something, something she could listen to, but if she settled herself down for a rest she clasped her hands in her lap and gave a deep sigh and seemed to be far away from them all. In the evening she sat and read the Bible or the Prayer Book, not aloud, but murmuring to herself. Then she would look pale and almost helpless over by the lamp, her small, thin lips trembling. But there was nothing special about her, nothing out of the ordinary. For people like her that's enough.

When the father came home at night he took off the jacket of his uniform, put out his signalling lantern and wiped it with waste; stood it outside in the passage, because it burnt whale oil and smelled after it was out. Then he would enter up car numbers for a bit and mention which were to be loaded and emptied next day, and something about the trains he had to see about. But when they'd finished eating he got the Bible and read it. There was a strange heaviness when they both sat reading and no one spoke. The children kept quiet; it was so silent that they felt weighed down. Down below was the third-class refreshment room, and from it came the noise and voices of people who were sitting there drinking. But that was something apart and outside them which they paid no attention to. Sometimes when a late train ran into the station the father went over to the window, stretched up and looked out, Bible in hand. Then he sat down again and went on reading.

The children were allowed to go out for a bit before bed-time. They crept along the dark corridor like a crew of mice, gradually raising their voices as they climbed downstairs. The spring evening shone and there was a smell as if it might have been raining. They crept through a little gate that led from the enclosed yard to the park. Then you heard the band, every kind of instrument drumming, piping and blaring. The flutes sounded out high and shrill; the trumpets struck in, booming. The park was lit up farther along.

They hurried in under the trees, darted among the trunks, crept as near as they dared. Right in front, there stood some old fir trees with branches sweeping down to the ground. It was quite dark there and they got inside, cautiously, being careful not to get resin on their clothes. The space in front streamed with light. There were lots of people listening to the band. The best of them had red rugs round them. The waitresses went about among the guests and poured out strange drinks. You could only see their white blouses above the tables; they floated between them like doves. In the bandstand, which was like the half of a house, the regimental band was playing in gleaming uniforms. The roof above it was a sky with golden stars. The instruments gleamed. The sound rolled out into the still night. Towards the end of a piece the big trumpet would have begun to drip.

The children stood breathless, their eyes moist and bright, not daring to stir. It was just as strange, remote and wonderful every time, although they had grown up with it.

Then when dusk fell they crept back home and were in bed dreaming about queer things they didn't understand.

But in the morning an old can of freshly strained milk was put in through the kitchen door. It came on a train that got in at 7:15, and stood by the driver on the engine. The milk was still warm and smelled of the udder; the children drank all they could get. Under the lid a slip was stuck in, wet because the milk had splashed. It said how the spring sowing was getting on, and the cows, whether anything had happened, or usually that there was nothing in particular, they were all right and everything was going as it should.

It came from the farm in the country; their home was there, where they had come from.

The children were dashing about in the park. It was so big that it seemed really like a wood, though one that was kept trim and cared for. All the same, in one corner it wasn't quite so tidy, the trees had sprung up every which way and the grass was left to grow just as it liked. That was where they liked to be. But they ran about almost everywhere. Over by the whitebeams that grew on the little hill close to the platform, in the abandoned fir grove with its heap of sardine tins and broken glass in the middle, and by the ant hill that stood a little way off where the quaking grass came right up to your knees as if the ants had manured it so as to hide their home from the world. And over at the other edge, too, where the lilacs were in flower the whole way along the street that bounded the park on this side. They were neither just playing nor going for a walk, but something in between. Sometimes they'd give a leap or chase each other among the bushes; then they would go along quietly listening to the birds chirping. It was a fine day, a wonderfully good day. A few wisps of cloud lay at rest in the sky as comfortable as could be. The sun came easily down, unhindered, and tended the growing things on the earth. You might well go about feeling content with everything as they did. The whole park really was their own now in the middle of the day. An old man was raking the paths somewhere so far away that you could hardly hear it where they were, and anyhow they knew him quite well, so it made no difference.

What about looking for lucky lilacs with five petals? That was a good idea. One of the girls was always finding these. As soon as she bent a branch down and began to search over a cluster she found several, even eights and tens. She was called Signe, and she comes in later. When she found a really big lucky one she felt uncomfortable because it was always hers. "Oh, I say . . ." she said, because she didn't know whether the others had found some, too. Then she clapped her hands and laughed and ate it; you had to do that to make sure it worked.

Then they began playing properly. The biggest boy clapped one of the girls on the back and ran and stood ready behind a tree. This was the beginning of tag, or old man, whatever you like to call it. They whirled about among the chestnuts and maples, in between the elder bushes where the earth hadn't been raked up, so that it didn't matter much running about there. It went on all over the park; now they were here, now there, sweating and out of breath. They caught hold of a branch for a moment and rushed on. The girls had to stop sometimes and let themselves be caught, but when they'd got their breath they flew off again.

Right in the middle of it they came quite close to the restaurant garden. They mustn't go there, but they stopped, panting, at the end of the paths that led down to it, stood and watched, the game brought to a standstill. It was queer to see how altered and desolate it all was in the daytime. The tables were bare and soiled, sticky with beer and *punsch* that had dried in and was smelling in the sun. Underneath them lay spent matches and chewed cigar stumps; in one place someone had been sick. The bandstand gaped empty and abandoned with the music rests shoved together like skeletons in one corner. Bits of the sky and the stars had fallen down. There was nothing cheerful or gay about any of it now; in the daytime they didn't care about it at all.

They set off again and took up the game where they'd stopped; the one who was "it" drove the others in front of him like a flock of wild sheep which scattered into the bushes. The girls' shrieks sounded like signals of distress from behind the trees. The flock whirled about through the whole park, from one side to the other, yelling in the blaze of the sun.

But the smallest, whose name was Anders, didn't join in. That didn't matter much though, because anyhow he wasn't able to run as fast as the others yet. He stayed where he was, looking wonderingly at the desolation among the dining tables, where at night everything had been so wonderfully lovely. Now it was like nothing; just grimy and laid waste. He had thought it was all really true; the sky and the stars, the brilliant lights, the bandsmen who were like angels, and the music that sounded so lovely that sometimes you daren't really take it all in. He remembered it all so well. And now—nothing was left, nothing was recognizable. How could a thing like that disappear and be just empty and desolate afterwards?

He was frightened, felt so weighed down that his chest would scarcely breathe properly. And surely he was shivering as he stood here, even though he was in the sun.

Sadly he walked up the path, looking down the slope. He heard the cries of the others up in the park, but he didn't want to go to them. Dawdled about by himself, didn't know what to do. Then he sat down on the big broad path that ran through the middle of the park and was gravelled the best; on the others there was earth just below the gravel, because there hadn't been enough, perhaps. First he poured sand over his shoe and patted it down, and when he pulled his foot out it made a little cave, like you have for potatoes or anything, anything that has to be kept. He made quite a lot of them, but it didn't take long, because he was good at that. Then he set about digging a really big hole. Scraped away with his fingers, deeper and deeper down, the sand got wet and fine, the hole so small at last that there was hardly room for his hand in it. He was so absorbed that he neither saw nor heard, and didn't notice that the landlord was about and not far off. Not until he was standing right over him and the shadow of his round paunch had fallen across the workplace.

The landlord was a kind old man, but the children were very much in awe of him, for they thought he owned everything in their part of the world. He didn't really own very much; he was only hiring it on a ten-year lease that wasn't up yet. He shook his head and played with the watch chain that lay in a wide curve over his waistcoat. "No, that will never do," he said. And so as to be really kind he added, "When little children dig holes it means that someone in the house is going to die."

He'd have spoken straight out to the other children, but

for one as small as this he thought he'd have to explain it somehow.

Anders started up white with terror. His face had gone quite stiff. He stared down into the hole; then he dropped down trembling on his knees and filled it up again.

The landlord thought there seemed something queer about him, and he took a bag of sweets out of his pocket. He liked children and he usually had some sweets for them. A sweet is always a sweet, and Anders with a trembling hand took a big, sticky one that was offered him. But when he'd said thank you he rushed away wildly, all among the bushes, across the lawns, up into the park.

Who was to die? Who was to die? Mother perhaps? Himself, perhaps? No, he was too small; he couldn't die yet. But Mother, she looked pale and sometimes said she felt tired. It surely couldn't be one of the waitresses; they all looked so rosy and well. No, it would be Mother—oh, if it were Mother!

He fell down in the grass, got up and rushed on again.

No, it was Father! Of course it was Father! He did shunting—and he'd be knocked down! It was Father it would be. He could see that now.

He dashed along. Where were the others? He couldn't be by himself, he must get to them! He couldn't hear them anywhere. Ah yes, there they were over by the white-beams. He scrambled up the slope, flung himself among them, white and panting, right into the arms of Signe.

The others didn't notice anything out of the ordinary, only that he came running all of a sudden. Signe saw it at once, lifted him onto her arm.

"What's the matter with you?" she asked.

He didn't know what to say. There were some things you couldn't tell, he'd noticed, and it wouldn't be worth it either, only make it worse; you'd got to put up with it yourself as well as you could. But he clung tightly to her.

The other children were leaning on the fence and looking down on the siding. There was a sheer drop; part of the hill had been blown away to make room for new lines. "Hi!" shouted Helge, the bigger boy, "there's Father!" They must all get a sight of him—yes, there he was standing on the footplate of the engine, holding on with one hand and waving to them with the other. Signe lifted up the smallest one as high as she could manage. Now their father jumped off and ran in under the buffers while the car was still moving. Anders stared down, hot with anxiety. They didn't see him, it took a long time. Signe felt Anders's fingers digging into her neck. At last their father came out again, signalled to the driver, and the cars ran in on their siding.

His sister put Anders down on the ground. He was shaking all over.

"That was perfect," said the big boy, who was leaning far out over the fence. "That's just where they ought to be. It's Johansson wants them for loading planks this afternoon.

"Well, what are we going to do now?" he went on, climbing down.

They stood discussing it for a while.

"I was going home to help Mother a bit," said Signe. And she took Anders's hand for him to come with her.

So the two of them left the others. They went down the lawn, past the skittle alley that rumbled as if it were thundering. A fat man came out in his shirt sleeves and puffed, a glass in his hand.

"Hell, what marvellous weather!" he said. "Morning, my dears."

They went along in silence, as if there were nothing they could say to each other. Signe could feel that his hand was still trembling, but she didn't know why. They came down under the trees, almost up to the gate into the yard.

Then his sister stopped short.

"You can have this lucky lilac, Anders," she said. And

she felt for one that she had put away in the pocket of her pinafore. It was a bit crumpled and cake crumbs had got in it. She blew on it to open it and get it clean.

"No, but you ought to have it yourself," he said.

"Oh, what does that matter? Just you take it. I'm always finding so many."

He put it in his mouth and went on in silence at her side, munching it up.

There was something special between Signe and her mother. You noticed that at once if you saw them together busy about the house, as they were every day. They seemed to have their life in common, a life that wasn't quite like the others, more important in some way. They seemed to be the heart that the others in their home listened for in order to know for certain that they existed. You could sit and listen to it in the kitchen, in the rooms, wherever they went about doing their everyday jobs; if they sat shelling peas out in the garden, if they were washing up, dusting, cleaning knives on Saturday afternoon.

Among the whole family there was an intimacy that kept them together and separated them from the outside world, but that was nothing to the bond between these two. They made one. There was nothing to distinguish them, except that the one was not yet as old as the other. It had to continue, not come to an end. That was why one was just a little girl and the other already a mother with many children, pale and worn, as one who had already lived most of her life. But now for a while they were both here at the same time and went about chatting to each other. Not that that made them solemn in any way, or out of the ordinary in their talk. No, it was never like that.

Take today for instance, when they're doing the washing in the kitchen. It's nothing out of the way; there's nothing unusual about it. They bustle around each other piling up wrung clothes, changing rinsing water, fetching the blue-bag, hanging stockings to dry out of the window, and now and again finding something to say, laughing a bit, then catching hold of the scrubbing boards and both getting serious again at the same time.

Signe is a plump little thing with a comical, shrewd look. She is golden-haired, her head all fluffy, her eyes sparkling. Just now she's sweating. She makes the soapy water hiss as she rubs the clothes, holds her head a bit on one side as if to get extra strength. Her face is red from her zeal. All over her hair little beads from the steam are glinting.

"Oh, I say, *Mother*," she says, stopping short. "Just *look!* How it's run!"

"Would you believe it?" says her mother. "I never saw such a thing. Let's only hope it hasn't gone on to the others. . . ."

"Oh yes, Mother. It's gone all on to the whites. Dear, oh dear, oh dear, what are we to do?"

"Oh, Signe, *what* a nuisance! Won't it come out? No, oh no. Well, there's nothing for it but to try and boil it out. That's what we'll have to do."

"Well, we do seem to be making a mess, I must say."

That's the way they talked, about anything that might happen. And they'd stand on their heads again over the washtubs, rinsing and wringing out.

The whole house lay silent and deserted, the sort of afternoon when it feels as if nothing will happen. Only up in the kitchen they worked for all they were worth at the washing. The sun went in and out on them, whenever the small clouds came and went up in the sky. The children were at school or away on their own.

"But what's Anders doing with himself?" asked her mother.

"He'll be sitting at the window," said Signe, "if there's no sign of him."

So he was. Sitting hunched up on the ledge and making drawings in the soot on the window sills. When he'd finished with one he'd move over to the next; there was one to each little window and the fine soot lay thinly everywhere. He didn't seem to see the trains that came in at the platform. But he *felt* them, gliding and gliding, changing and changing without break. He didn't need to see. Only when one moved off on the narrow-gauge track nearest the window he would lean out. It was much smaller than the others and looked so funny it made you laugh. It went off tooting and disappeared among the birches away to the right, puffing a bit of woolly white smoke up over the tops of the trees. He thought of it almost as his own train and waved to it a bit. Then he sat down again by his soot.

It seemed desolate and strange just now. The world seemed to have forgotten itself, didn't know what it was like. You could feel it over the houses across the platform, over everything. It all seemed to have stopped, to be everywhere empty and extinct. And he sat here drawing.

No, he didn't want to sit here any longer. Why shouldn't he go down into the yard and find something to play with? That would be best, that would make a change.

He climbed down and went across the room. Out in the corridor was the door into the kitchen. There he stopped, put his ear to it and listened. Mother and Signe were talking. What were they saying? You couldn't quite hear because they were scrubbing the clothes at the same time and the water was splashing in the tubs. It only sounded like a peaceful murmur. No, he wouldn't go in there. But he quite liked standing out here and listening a bit.

Now Mother said, "Signe, don't you think we might have a drop of coffee fairly soon? We've earned it now, haven't we?"

"Yes, Mother, I should just say we had."

"You get the pot ready, then. I'll finish the towels."

"Pfuh," said Signe, "it's fine to straighten up again." She laughed. And then began rattling the rings on the stove.

He crept away, down the dark stairs and out into the yard. It was enclosed by long, low buildings. The sun was blazing down just now, but he didn't seem to notice. The washing-up water was still standing in one of the gutters because of cork and lemon rind that had got into the grating. A bucket stood beside it with a bunch of withered carnations lying among coffee dregs and ashes. He went around the outhouses. On one side there were four doors to the closets. Away in the corner was a big pile of boxes full of empty beer bottles, there was a smell from the dregs. From there he went over to the other side, but keeping wide of an unpainted shed that had been put up in the middle of the yard. He didn't want to think about it. It had no windows, only a black hole in the middle of one wall. When you put your hand on it, it sent shivers all over your body. It was full of ice. No, he'd rather go and have a look in the woodsheds. The doors of all three stood open to let the wood dry. It smelled of birch, as if he'd stuck his head into a copse. In the end one stood a little old man sawing wood. He had a big white beard, yellowed with snuff under his nose, and small, peering eyes. Apart from that you couldn't see much of him in the half-dark.

"Hallo, nipper," he muttered. "What are you up to?"

"Nothing," said the boy.

"Yes, I can well believe it. But poor old Jonsson's sawing his wood. He's been doing that since he wasn't much bigger than you. From morning to night, day after day, until he's as old as he is now. Look how old he is. And all this drudgery just so that people shan't freeze to death. How many would have frozen to death, do you think, if poor old Jonsson hadn't stood here sawing wood his whole life long? Yes, many a thousand. Your father and your mother and Signe and the landlord and all the chits of waitresses—the whole lot of them would have frozen to death winters ago. But who thinks of that? Has anybody come and thanked me because he isn't dead? Not a single one. They don't think it's anything to say thank you for. But one day poor old Jonsson will have had enough of it. He'll be too tired and old and sick of it to toil for them any longer. And then the whole lot will freeze to death. Serve them right, eh?"

Anders just stood motionless and stared in at him.

"Well, anyhow, that's what'll happen to them. For it's bitterly cold in this world if you haven't got fires, I can tell you that.

"Well, well," he went on, "don't take that to heart. Out into the sun with you, my boy. Make sure you get warm while it's summer; then when it's winter we'll see what can be done." And he gave him quite a genial smile, strange to say.

The boy did as he told him, got out into the world and looked about him. There was really quite a lot of sun just now, the grass between the cobblestones shone freshly, and all along the gutter, where the crevices were richer, young dandelions stuck up. It was peaceful as a Sunday. If only he could understand why he had to feel so oppressed. It was like having a weight on his chest. Perhaps he might creep up and listen at the kitchen door again? No, he'd rather be down here. It was a fine day; you ought to be out enjoying yourself in some way after all. How was he to set about it? He really did want to, went up to the big carriage entrance and stuck his head out. There you saw a sunny patch of gravel and then a hawthorn hedge, and above them summer clouds that never moved. But apart from that there was nothing, only air, and up in that it looked all empty, as it sometimes does. He drew his head in again.

Well, perhaps he'd rather climb up into the ice shed. Perhaps that would be the best thing after all. Yes, that would be best, that's what he'd have to do.

He crawled up the plank that ran down steeply from the opening, gripped it fiercely so as not to fall off. He didn't dare to look up at the black hole, but kept his head down, crawled like a crab with his fingers around the edges of the plank. The cold that streamed out began to touch the back of his neck; then he got up to the opening. Jumped in as quick as he could, without looking.

Inside it was pitch dark. He groped his way in the wet sawdust, shivering all over with the cold. The lumps of ice were uneven. In some places more had been taken away and there were holes; in others it had piled up. At the edges the ice stuck out bare and made your fingers stiff.

He crawled about inside, tense, felt how cold it was, how dark, how terrifying. His heart thumped—no, he wasn't cold; his temples throbbed as if he were feverish. It was terrible. It was like being buried, not knowing whether you were alive or dead. You shook with terror. . . .

Who was it going along in the yard? It sounded like Father. . . . He crept up to the opening, looked cautiously out. Yes, it was Father coming home. He wanted to call out to him, to go with him up to the kitchen, to hold his hand up the stairs. He didn't want to be here—no, it would be best to stay here, it would be best for his father to disappear into the porch. He stood looking after him, with his mouth open, but without calling out.

How cold it was, how deathly and terrifying! Always the same dark and icy cold. He crept farther in; the cold seemed even worse there. His shoes sank into the wet sawdust; the walls and the roof were dripping with moisture. He stood still and seemed to let himself go rigid. Didn't move a hand, not a finger. Seemed carried away.

Why—how long had he stood like this? He had gone numb. Was he frozen, perhaps? No, his head was on fire, his whole body. He was overwrought—he must get out to the opening, breathe some real air and look down into the yard. He looked out, gasping, gripping tightly with his fingers, his head hardly above the edge, his eyes hot and frightened.

Just then his father came out again with a basket in his hand.

"Father!" he called, loudly it seemed to him, though he only gasped it out. It couldn't be heard down below. "Father!" he called again. Then his father looked up.

"Why, hallo, son, what are you doing there? You come down. What have you been up to? We've been looking for you. Don't you want to come along to Grandmother's? I'm going there on the trolley."

"To Grandmother's!" shouted the boy, waving his arms. "Wait, I'm coming, I'm coming straight away." And he scrambled down the plank on all fours as quickly as he could, rushed to his father, clung hard on his arm.

"Which trolley shall we have?" he panted. "Is it the overseer's or Karlsson's? We're going now, at once, aren't we—what have you got in the basket—is it for Grandmother—what is it—we're going right away, aren't we? . . ." He poured it all out without a break.

"What's the matter?" asked his father, looking at him. "What have you been doing up there?"

"Nothing," he answered, looking down. "I just stood in there for a bit. . . . Oh, I did want to come out with you. We are going right away, aren't we?"

"Yes, come along," said his father, taking his hand. They went out through the gate, out onto the gravel patch, into the sun. The child's breath came quickly, then more and more calmly. He looked about, up into the sky, down at the gravel which lay blazing yellow and freshly raked in the sun, at the hawthorn hedge which was almost white with bloom. Then, when they'd got a little way, he looked up inquiringly at his father, gave a pull at his arm.

"Won't it be fine going out on the trolley?" he said, with a rather shamefaced laugh.

"Why, yes, so it will," said his father. Then when they'd gone a few steps farther, Anders gave a jump into the air, ran ahead and opened the gate that led to the platform, ran down the steps to it, and then up again to fetch his father and have some company, out onto the line to walk on the rails, ran up and down, now in front, now behind.

"You seem in fine form," said his father.

"Yes, I think it's such lovely weather. Isn't it, Father? See how I can run on the rails!"

"Mind you don't fall!" his father called after him. Of course he didn't. In a moment or two he was back again.

"Where's our trolley, Father?"

"Oh, we'll find it all right. It's standing over by the warehouse."

And soon they came to the supply shed. There the whole tackle stood on end against the wall; a three-wheeler and a big pole to push along with, that was all, nothing out of the way. At first they had to be content to walk behind and push; only the basket rode.

"Shan't we get going soon?" Anders asked.

"Yes, as soon as we get past the points," said his father.

Anders ran ahead and made sure they were set right, so that the trolley shouldn't get upset with Grandmother's coffee and sugar and the bit of yeast that lay on top. Lifted the wheels if they got stuck. In his free moments jumped about at the side of the trolley.

Here all along the railway yard ran the town cemetery, with graves coming right up to the line. He didn't think about that, just looked the other way instead. It was rather a long way, the graveyard stretched out right to the end. But he had the basket and the trolley to see to, and the piles of planks at the other side to look at. And then he could talk to Father, too; it didn't take long. Now he knew that they'd come to where there were no more graves, only a few newly planted lime trees on a lawn; that was for those who were going to die, who were still alive. He pressed close against his father.

"Shan't we get going soon?" he whispered.

"Yes, just you wait a little while, son."

Soon after, out by the gates, they got going. Anders sat tight, holding the basket, his legs stretched out towards the little wheel. His father stood on the broad side between the two wheels and worked the pole.

They soon got up speed. They were far beyond the town in no time. The pole gave firm, even thrusts at the gravel, the wheels flew round as fast as they could go; over the joints they made a click like a real train. Although it was a still day, the wind went past them so fast that they had to pull their caps well down over their ears.

"Holding tight?" his father shouted to him, crouching down for speed.

"Yes!" he shouted back, looking up and laughing.

First there was a straight run through meadow land. The flowers rushed past like little dots. You couldn't see what they were; the smell from them all was thrown up against the embankment. Then they ran into the wood. A strong smell from the first was drawn past them and a smell of birches, light and fine, but still quite easy to tell, and of junipers and alders and pines; it was a mixed wood, a bit of everything. Then came a little of the wild strawberry smell, because they went past a patch high up on the embankment; they shone so red that you could see them for a long time, but past you went, you just went past everything. Down on the slope there were all sorts of flowers: marguerites, crow's-foot, buttercups, love-in-idleness, little tufts of clover which had strayed there, wild oats, raspberry canes, and lots besides. They all smelled and flashed out and rushed past, the firs, the birches, and the juniper bushes down in the wood as well. The telegraph poles fled backward as if they were running home, didn't want to come with them.

Anders sat with wide-open eyes, devouring everything; his cheeks were a little white with the rush of wind, but the excitement and rapture made him hot. His heart leaped and thumped. He seemed to be in ecstasy. His father rocked himself backward and forward to get the proper swing. He had to take care that the pole didn't go on the sleepers, otherwise it slipped; but things like that he did from pure habit and the speed got better and better.

Here the line curves to avoid the water. Here there's water on every side, lakes, rivers, streams, and ponds. Every now and again they came to a bit of bridge, where some stream had to go under. Then his father would give a really strong push, there was a roar and they were over.

"Mind you don't lose your cap!" he shouted down at the boy.

"All right!" Anders shouted back, holding on to the cap, the basket and everything. They went like the wind.

Now they passed the watchman's place at Näset; the children looked out in wonder between the lilacs, biting at their pinafores and curtsying. Soon they came to the big bridge over the river. There they had to pole themselves along on the sleepers with the broad current rushing under them. And then they had got to Näs station.

There they slackened speed a trifle, but not very much, because it was a small station with only one loop. The stationmaster was taking a walk along his station. He saluted just as if it were a real train, one that didn't stop at such small stations.

Then they got up their old speed again. It led past ploughed fields and clover fields, open land that belonged to a bigger farm and wasn't looked after very well, then into the wood again. It was a leafy wood that stood shining in the sun on both sides, full of the chatter of birds. Here eight men were at work on the line, changing sleepers that had rotted. They had a moment's rest while the trolley swished past. There had to be salutes in spite of the hurry, but Anders couldn't risk taking his cap off. He had to salute like his father, but with his head cocked on one side so that he could still hold the basket.

After that there was an incline, but they scarcely

noticed it at their speed. When you've got up it, the line makes a slope down right across the country. They call it the Street, and there you go for nothing, just flying along. Right on the crown of the rise was another watchman's place. The watchman was squatting against the chimney in the heat of the sun, tarring his roof.

"Hallo, what's the idea—an extra train?" he shouted down to them.

"That's all right, it's just us!" yelled Father into the wind, and by then they were already on their wild rush down.

His father pulled in the pole, keeping it ready to put a brake on the wheel if need be. The wind whistled past their ears. The little wheel at Anders's feet flew around so that you couldn't see the spokes. It leaped and skipped with joy. It was like a colt in the morning when it's first let out. The line ran on like a streak. Marguerites, buttercups, cowslips made single streaks as well, the straight line of the telegraph wires glinted in the sun, the sparrows on them darted in terror into the wood, where trees and bushes grew together into a smooth wall. A squirrel, frightened out of its wits, ran along the top of the fence as if it couldn't get inside.

The whole thing was over in a few minutes, the whole long hill. Then the country opened out on every side, with marshes, little lakes, ditches and streams, with tilled plots, open pasture, countless strips of ploughed land, with meadows, bogs and woods and farms scattered about among the oats and the rye out in the sun. It spread out so light and friendly that everything could be seen, and far off you could make out Grandfather's farm among its maples. They slackened speed. They rolled gently over a wide stream with rushes and water lily leaves at the edges, and shoals of bleak that leaped in the glitter. So they came to a rough village road that crossed the railway. There they slowed up and jumped off. They'd got there.

"We tore along, didn't we?" laughed the child, and ran around flinging his arms about. His father smiled contentedly and pulled the trolley down into the grass on the slope. Then they went through the gate and set off across country with the basket between them.

Anders was so elated that he could hardly make his legs walk properly. His father was in high spirits too and his walk was as easy as that of a young man of twenty. To brighten him up still more the boy pulled at the basket now and then; they both laughed at being out and walking together like this.

There was something strange about his father. It was as if he really were made for being glad. But it seldom came out, except when he was like this sometimes; he had something within him that was too heavy. He couldn't free himself from it and almost always went about serious and at times as if he were oppressed. He had worries, but it wasn't because of those. It was just that he was like that; he held back the lighthearted part of his nature as if it had been something wrong. His cheerfulness seemed to be quelled by his seriousness.

But now they were both of them gay and lively. The familiar fields lay on either side with all the growth in its summer fullness. Dust was rising from the rye and the air shimmered above the grey fences because of the heat. Their road ran a little way from the stream. They passed the mill and the miller stepped out big and mealy, just in time to exchange a word with them. Then they crossed a brook and after that went up a low hill; then they had the farm lying right below them.

It was high, with narrow gables. The red paint had almost worn off, and the grey planking showed through. The maples grew up over the roof, which was of turf, fine and old and covered with quaking grass. The cowshed lay on the other side of the road and looked old, except at the and where an addition had been made.

They hurried as fast as they could, watching to see whether perhaps someone was waving with the curtain. They couldn't see that, but a calf came scuttling along wildly to meet them, stretched its crumpled neck over the fence, sucked their fingers, and lowed. And just then the curtain began to stir. But now they'd got there and walked up through the garden.

It was full of apple trees, pear trees, lilacs and, right at the end, big flower beds, peonies, button dahlias, clear-coloured marigolds, tall hollyhocks, geraniums that had been put out of doors for the summer, stocks, lavender and mignonette that smelled a long way off. A low hedge ran along the path; Anders went on tiptoe to see over it into the currant bushes. But Grandmother was standing on the steps of the porch, among all her flowers.

"Well, children, so it's you," she said.

She was so old that she called them both children. Anders knew nothing so extraordinarily old. Her face was thin and worn, not wrinkled and yet full of furrows; her body short and strong, in a skirt that was as grey and dry as earth. And yet she was quite like Mother. Her eyes were the same, her hair just as fine, only hers was white. There was the same sensitive light about her, although she looked so dry with age. She took their hands, thanked them for all the coffee and sugar, which the boy had to show her at once. She pushed them ahead of her through the door and followed in stockinged feet.

Inside there was a strange smell of old wood and earth and dried manure which clung to the clogs in the porch. And from an upstairs room there came the smell of onions that were spread out on yellowed paper.

They lifted the latch and stepped into the big living room. It seemed almost in darkness when you came in from outside. Two big beds with skin rugs over them and a big table in the middle—that was the main part of the furniture; by the window stood a loom with linen for sheets on it. In the open fireplace an enormous copper kettle hung, for they cooked potatoes for the pigs. There his grandfather sat, looking after the fire. He was a strong man, although aged. He had a broad, large face, clean-shaven, the mouth set and without teeth. His hair fell down on his shoulders, long and white. He was dressed in moleskin trousers and a leather jacket with lead buttons. He didn't move, for his legs were stiff with age; waited for them to come to him.

"How are you, Grandfather?" said his father.

"God be praised," said the old man in a loud voice, for he was hard of hearing himself, "I've nothing to complain of. How are you getting on in the town?"

"All right, thanks. We're all keeping well," answered his father loudly and distinctly.

"And you, my little one, have you come such a long way with Father?" The old man lifted the boy onto his knee and fondled him a little with his big-veined hand. Anders, who always thought it was queer to be sitting here like this with his grandfather, looked at his heavy face, held on tight to the jacket; everywhere he was quite stiff to touch.

Father and the old man sat a long while talking together, loudly and slowly, so that the cottage echoed. There were one or two things his grandfather wanted to hear about. They spoke with the same seriousness about everything. If they touched on good news they still spoke seriously, as if it weighed on them. His father was altered. He sat with his hands clasped, his back bent a little, looking older, just as he did when he read the Scriptures at home in the evening. The smell from the potatoes spread out over the room. The windows got steamy.

His grandmother stole backward and forward between the kitchen and the small room. She could never rest, must always be doing and always had work enough to do. But she went in stockinged feet and you didn't hear her.

Now she came and tried the potatoes. They weren't done yet.

"But, Anders, why don't you go out to the currant bushes?" she said.

And he woke up, realized that it couldn't be right for him to be sitting here when they were so old, climbed down and crept cautiously out.

At first he was nearly blinded with all the flowers, especially with the peonies that were burning fiery red everywhere. The sun fell on the wall, and there the flowers stood wide open for bumblebees and honeybees that were crawling in and out, for gorgeous butterflies that just touched lightly on them, as if they lived on scent. He crept down among the currant bushes. The earth under them was warm and fine. The hens had been scratching there, hollowed out nests as if to lay eggs in, plucked out small feathers. He pushed aside the dry little droppings and sat down in a hole that was just the right size, thrust his arm up into the bushes and ate. The clusters hung all around. Some were bigger and sourer because they'd been in the shade; others out in the sun were small and sweet. In that way you could have a change, according to what you felt like. He considered carefully before he chose, because he meant to go on eating for a long time.

No one could see him or hear him where he crouched. And there was no one there who might have seen him, either; no one in the garden and no people on the road. It was peaceful and calm. Only a long way out on the marshes by the stream a cow bellowed now and again, and a few flies buzzed under the next currant bush. That was all. There was no wind. The maples were asleep in the sun; even the aspen, which should always be moving, stood still a little way behind him by the south gable. Now and then, so as to have a rest, he pushed aside a branch of his bush and looked up at the sky between the clusters and perhaps at a cloud that had stopped, that couldn't get any farther today.

But just when he'd eaten as much as he wanted, his grandmother came out onto the porch steps on her way with the potatoes to her pigs. She was looking about and listening for him, he could see—not that that was much good.

"Where have you got to, child?" she called. "Don't you want to come and feed the pigs?" But he crawled along noiselessly under the bushes, and jumped out on her near the gate instead and frightened her a bit. If it had been dark, of course, she'd have been really afraid, but it wasn't. They went on down to the cowshed.

The sow lay heaving in the sty with the little pigs at all her dugs. She hung down into the muck even when she got up, but from out of her fat she gave grunts of pleasure; the little pigs rolled off her in every direction. She slobbered up the whole troughful at a stretch; the little ones tried to get at it, too, but they weren't big enough to reach it yet. Then he and Grandmother went on and saw to things in the cowshed. There was mucking out the oxen, and then a cow that had been brought in because it was going to calve. The hatches out to the dungheap had to be opened. There was none too much manure in the summer when it all went to waste out in the pasture; there was hardly more than a puddle that the sun shone down into. The cow that was in calf turned heavily in the stall and lowed, looking out through the opening. Now a hen let out a screech from up in the loft.

"She's laid, I expect," said the old woman. "Go and look for it, Anders!" And he climbed up the ladder.

He stayed up there in the dark awhile, tumbling in the hay that smelled so good. It was newly brought in, loose; you fell about everywhere. It was dark here, but of course that didn't matter. The only light came in through a hole. He went and looked out through it for a bit, his legs hanging and dangling a little. He found the egg, and another one in a different nest.

"Those can be for Mother," said Grandmother.

It was good to be going about with her, seeing to things and now and again chatting a bit. She was grave and wise, but so kind that you didn't really notice it. It was just like it was with Mother. And when you went about with her you seemed to see everything so clearly, and that made you feel secure in a special kind of way.

When they'd finished it was time to go out on the marshes for the evening milking. It was getting towards evening, though the sun was still warm. It was wet out there, so that they had to go barefoot. Anders followed Grandmother's big feet on the tussocks; they looked old and they had thick corns from the clogs. The cows came to meet the two and let themselves be milked quietly, but Anders had to hold their tails to stop them from flicking; the horseflies gave them no peace.

It was lovely out here, although the land was poor. You could see right across the parish along the stream that ran through it. The country lay resting, and the farmhouses cast long shadows towards the stream. There was no high land anywhere there, but it was relieved with meadows, wooded rises and tilled plots. Down here in the dip the ground hardly seemed to rise above the level of the stream, and farther in on the marsh there were black holes where skaters darted all over the sunny water. It was a real summer day; it made the smallest insect happy.

As they turned home with the milk there was a rumbling away in the west and the air seemed close. His uncle, who looked after the farm, had come in from the wood with logs and was now putting up the oxen. It was fine to meet him. He was blue-eyed and fair, a middle-aged man, thickset and strongly built, but you could tell that he was used to hard work. When you shook hands with him it felt stiff like touching bark; he'd lost a finger at a wedding once when they were letting off a gun in salute. He let them help him unyoke the oxen and drive them into the stall. He was rather silent tonight, tired perhaps. You could hear his breathing, as you can with people who do heavy work.

Then they all three went up through the garden. The thunder rumbled again and it felt oppressive. He couldn't understand why it should have got close; there had been nothing but fine weather all day. His father and grandfather still sat in the dimness of the cottage, resting. Now they were all to have supper.

The old woman blew the fire up and put on some pork in the frying pan; laid out plates and the other things they wanted. The men talked. There were gusts in the maples down the garden and at the same time it grew dark indoors. The old woman stood the frying pan on the table, on two split logs; there was a fine smell and a sizzling from the pork. At that the old man got up and said grace in a loud voice. They sat down gravely as if subdued by the words, helped themselves and ate.

They didn't speak at all while they were eating. The old woman sat a little way off, at the other end of the table. Now and again she slipped out into the dark kitchen and came pattering back again. A flash of lightning lit up the room. They looked up and sat waiting. The rumble came long after.

"We oughtn't to have a fire," said the old woman.

"It's a long way off," answered his uncle, and helped himself to more.

The trees swayed down again; it was so silent that outside you could have heard every leaf. The hollyhocks beat against the pane; then the windows flashed out again. The rumbling sounded louder. Immediately afterwards came another flash.

"It's about time I was getting home," said his father, who was on duty that evening.

"As long as you don't get into the storm," said the old woman.

"That can't be helped. And perhaps I can miss it."

Anders had better stay here overnight, he decided. "We'll come out and fetch you tomorrow."

It seemed strange to the child not to stay with his father. To stay here by himself, that wouldn't be bad, perhaps. . . . But here wasn't quite what it had been a moment ago. He'd rather go home. No, that wouldn't do, they decided.

They finished the meal and his father said good-bye. Anders watched him go from the one to the other, following him with his eyes. After that he followed him out onto the porch steps and stood looking after him. The garden was gloomy and desolate. The big maples were grey because the leaves were turned over by the wind. Now his father disappeared over the top of the rise. It seemed so queer.

Would he ever see him any more?

A terrific flash lit up the whole landscape, far out over the marshes, the heather slopes and the ploughed fields—the earth looked all grey and dead, the sky was flaming. He ran inside, the door slammed behind him with the wind, he wrenched open the door into the room and got inside, white and stiff with terror. Then came the thunderclap, crashing on every side; the windows rattled. The old man by the hearth raised his head, looked around out through the windows.

"It's good, hearing it thunder," he said; "then you understand that God's is the power."

That said, he got up shakily and slowly and fetched the Bible.

"Where's my hairbrush, Stina?" he said.

The old woman found it, a small homemade round horsehair brush with twine binding for the handle. He brushed and dressed his hair till it lay neat and white down to his shoulders. Then he undid the clasps of the big Bible, opened it and began to read.

"'Hear ye, and give ear; be not proud: for the Lord hath spoken.

"'Give glory to the Lord your God, before he cause darkness, and before your feet stumble upon the dark mountains, and, while ye look for the light, he turn it into the shadow of death, and make it gross darkness.'"

He raised his voice still more when he read. Every word sounded out loud and distinct in the room. The old woman crept about listening, her short body drawn together; she stood oppressed and sighed. His uncle sat by the window and looked out. The whole room flamed out with a flash, the trees outside stood out distinctly; the crash came at once. The old man didn't stir, went on reading.

His grandmother had cleared away now and she also took a chair so that she could sit and follow better. Nobody moved. The flashes of lightning darted between the windows. Then the rain came, streamed down the panes; the claps of thunder came one after the other, it was right overhead.

The boy kept on the move, sat crouched by the loom, crept out and sat by the table, then over in the corner by one of the beds, according to how the lightning might be going to strike. The others sat still and listened. All the time he kept his eyes fixed on the old man. The furrowed face never changed, the forehead was almost smooth, but on the cheeks and around the big mouth the furrows cut deeply in, as if he had been ravaged by a long life. It's true enough that in his prime he'd led a wild life, lived hard, but there was no need to speak of that, and Anders knew nothing of it. But all through his youth, and again when he'd got old, he had lived only to fear God and let himself be led on his way. He had a peace that nothing could ruffle.

The thunderstorm passed over, sounded farther and farther off. He went on reading. The old woman watched him with clasped hands, following the movements of his mouth.

The rain left off; you could only hear the trees outside. The clock on the wall struck nine. At that he put aside the book and looked up.

"Amen, in the name of God Almighty, Amen."

Anders came forward steathily. . . . Now they'd go to bed. His uncle, who slept in the little room upstairs, said good night and went. The child was alone with his grandparents, who were so old; he would be sleeping with them. It seemed strange. They undressed; he had to help his grandfather to pull the trousers off his stiff legs. The old man fell on his knees beside the bed and said the evening prayer in a resounding voice. The old woman had to help him to his feet again; then they both lay down with a skin rug to keep them warm, even though it was summer.

Anders was soon ready and crept into the bed by the other wall. It was so large that he was lost in it; the stiff skin rug came up to his chin, pressed on him when he breathed.

With wide-open eyes he lay staring up into the darkness so as to get to sleep. It was dark everywhere, in the garden, down by the stream, far out on the marshes, and darkest of all in here where he lay alone with the two old people. He listened—there wasn't a sound. They'd be asleep now. The maples made no sound either; not one of the trees anywhere. But in here it was quietest of all. Only his heart was thumping.

He thought about Grandfather and Grandmother lying over there, how old they were. They were all wrinkled, they were so old. And they had an old smell, different from his—he thought he could tell it even from here. Everything here had a smell: the straw in the bed he was in, the rough bedticks; the sheep's wool lying in a heap under the loom; the broad, worn floor planks with black caulking in between; the soot in the open fireplace that gaped into the room; the earth clinging to the clogs in the porch. Everything had an old smell. Everything was old, old.

And he not asleep? His heart thumped. He felt as if he couldn't breathe; the rug pressed down on his chest. He was so hot. . . .

Hsh! . . . No, not a sound.

Why couldn't you hear the old people, their breathing? You could hear *him* clearly enough, hear him panting. . . .

Could he really not hear them? No, everything was silent! Weren't they breathing?

Were they dead? *Perhaps they were dead!* Old as they were, with their end so near, it might come at any time. *Perhaps they were dead!*

He must get up. In the dark. *They were dead!* He groped his way—across the floor—up to the bed—stretched out his hand—felt his grandfather—his wrinkled throat—his gaping mouth. . . .

No, they were both safe and sound asleep.

He crept back, got into bed. Tiredness overcame him and he fell asleep. At times he turned over restlessly, sighed deeply. He dreamed that it was dark everywhere, in the garden, far out on the marshes, in the woods, over the station, at home, everywhere. And the darkness was a great black grave, where all the dead lay and all the living, too. And overhead in the flaming sky a mighty, thundering voice spoke incomprehensible words over both living and dead.

One autumn day, when he was twelve years old, Anders was on his way to a stone he had in the woods outside the town. It was raining and blowing, not hard, but about as much as it does in the autumn. He kept to the railway line. From where they lived that was the natural way if you wanted to go to the woods. In the station he saw his father noting down the cars; he was stooping a bit and his back was wet with the rain. He slipped along on the other side of the cars so that his father shouldn't see him, he might wonder where he was off to in weather like this. Hearing his father's steps when they got opposite each other, he walked quietly himself so as not to be heard.

He hadn't really thought it would be necessary to go out there today, but there it was, he was going. He hadn't remembered this, had other things on hand. Besides, it had been fine weather at first, and he used not to go out there on fine days. But later on it came into his head, and he realized he'd better.

There was a drizzle, but he didn't hurry. Serious and somehow weighed down, his hands deep in his pockets, wearing a skimpy little jacket with yellow buttons. An engine was shunting, made a nice warmth as it went by.

Yes, in the morning it had been quite clear, though it was chilly. He had been up early, by six o'clock, because the sailors had come by the train, fifty boys on their way to the naval station down on the coast. They wanted coffee, and on the space in front of the railway restaurant long trestle tables had been laid. They yelled and bawled with their mouths full of bun; there was the smell from the steaming coffee in the chilly morning air. And they waved to the children up at the little windows—perhaps they thought it was funny to see them hanging out up there. Stuck their quids in their mouths and got back into the train.

Things like that you got to know about the night before, so that you could get up and look at them. Afterwards he'd gone to sleep again for a little while and then gone to school. In the hour he'd had plenty to do with homework, besides getting some paraffin for Mother. He hadn't thought about this. He never did think of it, before it had to be. The weather changed, like it was now. After school he'd helped young Gustav to carry the chairs in from the restaurant garden; they'd got to be put away till next season, stacked in the skittle alley, which was being shut up. Gustav had a last shy. Then he'd gone back home to his own things, stood listening a little while outside the kitchen door because mother and Signe were talking in low voices about something. He thought it was about his being ill, perhaps that he couldn't live very much longer. He'd been listening for that word for about a year now, although he couldn't feel as if there were anything wrong with him. He got up by the window and looked at the trains shunting backward and forward in the rain. It was then that he realized that he'd have to go out to the stone for a bit today. It was such a heavy day. This had to be, that he knew. He was bound to do as it said.

Now he was by the sheds at the far end of the station. An engine was standing there being coaled up; that was fairly warm, too, as he went past. But after that he was out on the line, where there were open fields on both sides. The rain came driving in the wind, up over the high embankment, squally and swishing—you could see the wind blowing it. He bent his head and braced himself when the gusts came. It was worst here. But it *had* to be hard. It had to be like making a sacrifice.

What they'd been speaking about in low voices, of course it might perhaps be something else. But what could it be? Sometimes he'd noticed that he'd made a mistake, that really they hadn't been speaking, had just been sitting silent. But today surely they'd been whispering. Why did they lower their voices, if not because they thought he was going to die soon? If it weren't that, why couldn't they talk out loud?

The wind drove greyly across the fields; the sky hung low. Now he got to the wood and the wind dropped; there was just rain. The water was dripping from the trees, down into the moss and the whortleberry clumps. It was grey there; the firs dragged their branches, hadn't strength to hold them up, they were so sodden. You were looking down on it a bit from up here on the embankment. He went on; it wasn't far to go now. There were drops running along the telegraph wires, but they went the other way, towards the town. He walked on the sleepers; they were tarred, didn't hold the water, it just stood in beads on them.

Now he'd got there, climbed down the embankment, through the fence and into the wood. The rain showered down from the trees when he squeezed in and brushed against them. Here it was getting dark already because of the bad weather; it wasn't really late. A little way in among the tussocks lay a flat stone that only stood out a few inches above the earth. There was nothing unusual about it. The only thing that could have been thought remarkable was that a stone should have been there at all. Except for that one there weren't any; it was all spongy, mossy earth. He looked about him cautiously, towards the railway line, though no one would be likely to come there. Then he lay down on the stone and prayed.

It was silent all around, only the trees dripping. He made no sound either, didn't pray out loud, but his cheeks glowed. Straight in front was a boggy opening in the wood, and in the middle of it stood a stunted pine, hardly the height of a man, irregular and badly grown. He looked at it the whole time, though it wasn't to that that he was praying; it was simply what he always did. No, he prayed to the same God as they did at home; there was no difference. But it was his way out here. He didn't know why. It had just happened like that. Not for the sake of praying close to nature—there was nothing solemn about that for him, on the contrary. And yet. . . . It was no use trying to pray at home; it didn't come ardently enough there, it was too slight in faith and not vehement enough to be heard. So much was required to make sure of being heard. And that was why it was no use coming here on fine days, when you'd be glad to be going for a walk. He might almost as well not do it at all. No, he didn't really know—he felt it was hard and strange that he should have to come out here; it often made him suffer. But of course it had to be hard. It must be.

There was a way set for him. He had a world to himself and lived in it, a narrow world with ideas and precepts that must not be violated, never questioned. It was like being in a sort of cellar in broad daylight; he groped his way. Nothing could be done about it. It *was* so.

His cheeks burned more and more. He lay with his hands clasped tight. But he had only a single prayer: Let him not die, let none of them die, for certain, not one. Let Father live, let Mother, let his brothers and sisters—he went over them—the old people in the country, all of them, all! Let not one possibly die. Let everything be as it was. Let nothing be changed!

His whole passion for life was bent on its not coming to an end. He asked no boon beyond that. Only to live. Apart from that, things might go as they would. It didn't matter. It couldn't be helped.

Yes, he really insisted that apart from that things might go as they would, so as really to show how little *that* mattered. In that way surely he'd be more certain of getting what he did ask for, that which alone mattered. He half-shut his eyes, *thought* hard of everything he said, so that he actually *saw* it—it was as though he held it out, prayed and prayed that all might be as it was, that it should never come to an end. That it should be winter now, that it should be summer again next summer, that it should continue, continue—and that he and all of them should be there in the midst of it.

He worked himself up into an ecstasy, more and more fervent and intense, till it had full possession of him. It sounded inside him like an anthem to life, a strange anthem which never grew into an exultant song, which only counted everything up, only held despairingly fast to everything. But still it seemed an anthem.

In the space in front of him the rain was drizzling down,

falling into the greyish yellow moss and on to the tree that he was staring at. But it was quite silent in here, as dark as if it were evening already. In its own way it was solemn lying there and praying on the stone in the half-dark. He didn't stir, not even his mouth; only his burning cheeks, and his fingers clenched as hard as he was able.

After the prayer he got up quickly. Relieved, as if he were glad it was over, he rubbed his knees where they had got wet.

He jumped across onto a tussock, and then to another. He was on well-known ground here, but it was really wet today. Anyhow, on the tussocks it wasn't too bad. The fir branches hung drenched with rain that stood in drops among the needles. The alders stood with slender glistening branches. There were still leaves on the low birches in this sheltered place; they made the trees into big yellow fires and lay burning among the heather and moss as well.

How fine it was to be alive, just alive a little, for a short time. He wouldn't die now at once, not today, not even tomorrow. No, not now when he'd just finished praying that he should be allowed to live. The birches and the red whortleberry clumps, the delicate heather bells all met him with, "Well, my child, so here you are going about and living. And what are you up today?"

He hopped about on the tussocks like a young bird, looked up into the trees, thought he heard something, squirrels, perhaps? Shook a fir branch and let it pour down on the whortleberry clumps; spared a little of the downpour for some cloudberries which he would be gathering another time. Then he clambered up on to the embankment again.

He went more briskly now. The drops on the telegraph wires were running in the same direction, homeward bound as well. He looked around, up at the treetops and the clouds all around. The weather had cleared up quite a lot, stockdoves cooed in the wood, other birds broke into twittering.

He stretched out his hand. Perhaps it was still raining after all? No, it wasn't. The sky stretched away, broken and sparse, as though if it liked it could open itself out. Sparrows came out onto the wires, sat and shook the rain off themselves.

Yes, the world was all anyhow. This way or that way, there was no knowing. It was just as chance would have it. It wasn't worth wishing anything in particular for it, that was clear. So long as you had a chance to exist, a chance to be about. And he still had that after all.

He kept on; came out into the fringes of the wood, where there were two cellars which the ironmongers from the town kept gunpowder and dynamite in; thought what a crash there'd be if they went up; came out into the open fields. It wasn't quite so windy now; from the embankment you could see clearly in every direction. He came to the sheds and into the station. A little scattered shunting was going on. The engines whistled and puffed out their smoke; the two narrow-gauge engines piped thinly like young birds, spat and hissed in their cylinders as they fetched up the coaches for the evening trains; the proper big one on the wide track flung its smoke into the sky in dignified clouds. Station men leaned out from vans and timber cars as they ran free, waved and signalled with their arms. One engine had five open cars of whortleberries behind it; one came panting with a long line of lowing cattle cars. It was a lively place right enough. He picked his way among the trains, crossed the tracks according to the lines they took, said hallo to firemen and drivers, station men and the brake boys with lanterns on their way to the trains; thought of one thing and another, felt really bucked up. . . .

What had set him off on all that? All that about dying. He wasn't going to die! No more than anyone else. Not till later on, and that was the same for them all. Might leave that to look after itself.

He'd got over it for the time being. His heart felt light; he was back again among the others. People were walking up and down the platform with cases in their hands. Old women came rushing along, thought they were going to miss it. Olsson in the luggage van rang the first bell, Karlsson ran the luggage out, shouted to people who were in the way; the fireman lit the lamps on the front of the engine for the journey out into the world.

He climbed up the steps of the restaurant opposite, back home again. From the third-class refreshment room came the shouts of two drunks whom the train was going to leave behind. But inside the yard between the woodsheds it was already quiet. He crept upstairs, along the dark passage. Outside the kitchen door he stopped and listened a little while—no, there were none of them sitting and whispering. He hung up his jacket out here in the dark, because it had got wet, and crept in.

There was Mother; she was getting supper ready. They chatted a bit. He could see that she thought he'd been up in the park for a while. For his part he was cheerful and bright, talked about the sailors that morning and Gustav's last shy before the skittle alley was shut up for the year. His mother went about within the light she always spread around her, calm and peaceful. To him she seemed grave.

Then his father and the rest of them came in and they had their meal. The lamp was lit in the room and Father and Mother sat at the table reading the word of God, while his sisters made the beds, quietly, whispering; you scarcely heard them. He sat hunched up at the windows. It began to rain again, beat against the panes from the darkness outside. The last trains whistled and went off, the glow of their furnaces in the sky. But here indoors it was quite silent and still. Only his mother sighed at times and her lips trembled as she read. It oppressed you, it was as though she needed help, as though she were alone.

How everything weighed down on them here at home.

One morning the milk can didn't come alone. Grandmother got off the train with it in her hand, dressed for Sunday, in her old, fine kerchief. She stepped over the rails, looking about her carefully, and went up to the restaurant, where the waitresses were lolling at the windows, looking for guests. She curtsied to those she met. She seemed almost smaller here in the town. Her dress was black, but the folds were grey with age, not with having been worn. The skirt reached down over her feet, so that they were hidden, and it was so stiff that it hardly moved as she walked. The black silk kerchief was a wedding present; it had roses stamped into the material. It was so large that she was almost lost in it. The fringe fell down over her shoulders; her old firm chin stuck out over the knot. Instead of a coat she had a brown shawl wound around her and tied at the back. It was wintertime, frosty and clear, slippery underfoot. She walked easily for her age, only a little stiffly because of the shawl; looked up at the turrets and battlements of the house, the snowed-up niches and balconies—no one could be seen at the small windows above the third class. No, she was not expected. By the gate a drift had gathered during the night; she had to step over it. In the courtyard, which smelled of beer, she curtsied to the landlord and young Gustav, who was shovelling snow away, went into the passage and up to the family. When she knocked on the kitchen door the youngest children came and opened it. They were washing themselves, just going to school. Mother was there cooking porridge. No, no one knew at all that she was coming.

"God bless you, my dears," she said, and sat down, a bit tired. "I've come with the milk. Why, that's just right; I see you're going to have porridge."

Mother helped her off with her shawl. The old woman seemed small in the chair; the flannel bodice lay drawn in and wrinkled against her breasts. She took the kerchief off too. The fine white hair shone, and the kind eyes—eyes that were sunk deep in, as they are in old people. Well, everyone at home wanted to be remembered. They were getting on well, thank God. Uncle Emil had a lot of wood-carting with the oxen to do; he was hard at it, poor boy. It's slow work without a horse. Grandfather was keeping all right. And the cows were yielding well; there was still plenty of feed. Yes, God was very good to them all. Now next week they were going to kill the pig. Ah, of course, they'd said that in the letter with the milk day before yesterday.

But why had Grandmother come into town like that without letting them know?

Well, they'd thought she'd better come on. She'd been against it; she didn't think there was any need for it. It was just that she hadn't felt quite well lately, nothing to speak of, but still they thought perhaps she ought to see what the doctor said. It was they who wanted it, not that there was any need for it.

Mother sat down beside her and took her hand. They all grew quiet. They all looked at her. She seemed the same as usual. Well, perhaps bent a little more. And her face was thin, perhaps. But then it always had been. It was extraordinary how deep her eyes were sunk in. But then they often were in old people. Yes, she seemed the same as usual.

But Mother patted her hand, asked what was the matter, where the trouble was.

Why, it was only just that she didn't feel quite well and got tired at her work, so that she couldn't get on with it. But she hadn't any pains, nothing to speak of, well, perhaps a little ache. No, it was nothing. But it was the ones at home who wanted it. And perhaps she could have some medicine so that she could get along all right with her work again.

She folded her hands and looked at them, looked to see how they were, smiled at them a little, though not like she used to, perhaps. Mother was grave as she sat beside her, didn't take her eyes off her. They were like two sisters, they were so much alike. It was the paleness and the fine hair, the features which had the same sensitiveness and calm. They were so much alike in build, too, wiry and short. Mother stroked the old woman's hand a little; she wouldn't care to show more because of the children standing round. They'd got to remember that Grandmother was old, she said; she'd soon be seventy-eight, things couldn't be the same as before. Yes, now they'd go up to the doctor together, as soon as he was open, that's what they'd do. And then Grandmother would soon be right enough again.

"It's in God's hand," said the old woman.

The children stared at them, silent and wondering—it was extraordinary how grave Mother was. Anders stood farthest off, his face white, gazing at his grandmother as if he wanted to see right through her. They didn't talk any more. The girls looked for something to do out in the kitchen, put out the plates and porridge for the two youngest, who'd got to get off. Anders had to come up to the table and eat—he couldn't get anything down; said good-bye as soon as he could and crept out through the door with a long look at the old woman.

He and his sister ploughed along through the snow on their way to school. It was frosty and unnaturally quiet, the town was deserted, there were no footprints leading from the steps of the porches. It was as if no one lived in the houses. They walked one behind the other without saying anything.

The bell began to ring in the tower—Anders gave a start—were they going to ring the church bells? No, it was only striking half-past.

They could hear children in the other streets. They came tearing along in twos and threes, yelling and shoving. Down on the church piece they found their slides again under the snow, took a run and went off in a long string, fell down and got up again. Anders and his sister kept behind, did short little slides without taking a run, as if they didn't belong with the others today.

There were two lessons before they stopped for lunch. Anders sat trying to follow the words that were read, to hang on to them and not be alone, to be among the others. But he couldn't lose himself in it. While he listened intently, made himself hear how it went, *thought* how he was sitting here and listening—still he was miles away from it all.

What were they talking about? It just struck the walls, from one side to the other, and meant nothing at all.

And then they talked about God—here, too, here and at home, everywhere! Who was he? What was the point of all this talk? Did they suppose it helped?

No, he'd no use for God. It wasn't the same as before. And he never had seen much in him really—he didn't come into this.

No, if he could run out into the wood, if he could get off for an hour and run out there as hard as he could, rush off before it was too late, run, run, so that he got there completely exhausted, panting and feverish, and then fell across the stone. . . .

If he could get off, say he *must*, say there was something more important than anything, that he had to tear off. . . .

No, no one would understand. What could he say? That he had to run out into the wood! Who would understand that he had to? That you must beg and pray on your knees, fervently, really fervently, on a stone . . . pray that they might live. . . .

He worked himself up, didn't know what was going on around him; didn't notice they'd had a break, come in again, got another teacher. They seemed now to be talking about something else. . . .

Yes, they talked about so much. It was as if they didn't realize that only one thing mattered. They were always thinking of something else. Not that they were going to die, that they were going to die. . . .

Then the bell went and they were let out, fought and shouted in the corridor. In the playground they threw snowballs at each other's heads, the last ones before lunch.

Anders and his sister went home silently. They didn't know whether to hurry or go very slowly. Towards the end they almost ran.

But Grandmother wasn't back from the doctor yet. There were only their brothers and sisters, sitting waiting.

Anders climbed up by the windows, sat down and watched, crouched, as if to spring. His heart thumped, his eyes were hot as if he were feverish.

Then they came walking along, Mother and Grandmother up the path, calmly and quietly. They were both old women, both in kerchiefs, but Mother wearing a coat with braid. They said good morning to one of the station men, to the cook who was lolling out of the kitchen window in the restaurant, then disappeared into the doorway. They came into the room and were met by all the children, sat down and talked.

There was nothing to be done for Grandmother. No, it was too late. The doctor had examined her carefully and been so nice and kind. But there was no help for it. It was cancer and had gone too far.

"Well, well," said the old woman, "God's will be done."

Mother told it all, not the old woman. She only put in a word occasionally.

It was extraordinary, she said, how good and kind he was with her. She'd always heard that he was so stern with people; they often shrank from going to him. But with her he'd sat talking as kindly as if she were a child. And he wouldn't let her pay anything, didn't think she could afford it. She thought that was really kind of him. In the ordinary way he'd have been very dear, he had so many qualifications. Yes, he was really nice.

The children stood around them, crying. Behind, out of the way a bit, stood Anders, pale as death, his face frozen and thrust forward, just staring at the old woman. She was sitting with Mother under the windows which were frosted over with the cold. They didn't take it as anything dreadful. Why, Mother seemed to be transfigured in some way, just as if she were not really there. But she patted Grandmother's hand almost the whole time and did little things for her, folded her kerchief, put the folds right in her skirt. Something had been changed between them—Grandmother was like a child which her wise mother took care of and looked after. The old woman seemed somehow perplexed by what had happened to her, sometimes absorbed by it as if it were an external event. Sat stroking the kerchief that lay in her lap, the fine wedding kerchief with the roses stamped on it. Then it seemed to occur to her that the children might be asking themselves how long she would still be living among them. And she said that she'd asked the doctor that, because she wanted to know how things were, so that when her time came she could be ready. But he had turned away and said he didn't know. She understood him then and was sorry she'd asked.

"No," I said to the doctor, "*we* know nothing about that."

The trains puffed and whistled outside; it was getting towards the time when there was most shunting. The smoke swept over the windowpanes so that the ice thawed. Mother said it was time for a drop of coffee. "Yes, that would be very nice," said the old woman; the girls went to get it ready.

Then they sat around the table, drinking it, not saying very much. The children sighed, bent over their cups;

sometimes one of them had to get out a handkerchief, cry on the quiet. Anders wouldn't have any, kept on walking about, tiptoed on the rugs all round them, up to the windows and back again to the door, his face white. His eyes were quite dry, somehow lustreless. Once the old woman met his frozen glance and nodded, smiled at him a little. But his face didn't change at all and he couldn't look her in the eyes.

When they'd finished coffee the old woman got up.

"Now I must get back home to them. You'll come out and see me, won't you, my dears?"

Then it broke out; the children couldn't hold their crying back. Mother had tears in her eyes, too, but she didn't cry.

"Yes, Mother dear," she said, "we'll come now even more than we did before."

"It's kind of you not to forget us," said the old woman.

It was the first time death had come near them at home; that was why it gripped them so hard. They felt how completely they belonged together, couldn't realize that one of them could go, could be lost, not be among them any more. All the warmth they had in them broke out and made them feel one, more than ever before. But it strengthened them and helped them in their distress.

Only Anders seemed to be outside the warm stream that ran through them. He crept a little way into the other room and watched them from there without a tear in his eyes. The children came up and patted the old woman awkwardly. But not he. It was as if he didn't love her as much as the others.

"I've one or two jobs to do in the town," said the old woman, while they helped her on with her shawl, fastening it at the back. She had to go to the ironmonger's and get some nuts for the chaff-cutter. And then Emil wanted a quarter of snuff from Lundgren's—he says he likes theirs so much better. And they must have a pound of coffee, too, for when they killed the pig next week. Mother asked her to promise not to be there when they killed it; she wouldn't be able to stand it, you got so cold. But she brushed that aside.

"You know I've got to be by. I'm not in such a bad way yet."

"What I can't see," she went on at the door, "is how they're going to manage when I'm gone. It comes so dear having a stranger—they can't run to that."

She tied her kerchief and arranged it on her head.

"Well, now I'll be going. And thanks for everything."

So she went off again with the milk can in her hand.

Grandmother lived another year. In the summer she was able to help with the haymaking, and a little when they brought in the rye, too, but after that she had to stay in bed. They often went out and saw her between one train and the next, heard how she was getting on. Anders wouldn't go. He would make one excuse or another and they usually let him stay at home. Still he had to go sometimes. As they got nearer the farm he went paler and paler. When they came in and he had to take her hand, it was as if he could hardly do it. He would hardly look at her, not in the eyes. The others were just as usual, wouldn't show anything, just treated her specially kindly. To him it was as if she'd already changed, as if she were already dead. Sometimes she gave him a long look. Perhaps she thought that he wasn't so attached to her as she'd believed.

As soon as he could go he crept out; walked down the paths in the garden. The flowers had no scent—none of all these flowers of Grandmother's. He moped along by the currant bushes, remembered how he used to lie under them, in the blazing sun—and then she would come out on the steps. He looked in the arbour, where she used to sit shelling peas; it was like a great empty hole. Everything was changed, nothing was like it used to be. And yet the sun shone, as if it were midday and the height of summer. But now everything here was *marked.* It was not real.

He scrambled through the hawthorn hedge and stood looking over the countryside. It was absolutely empty. The grass fields lay there, the stony land with fences round it, and the farms lay scattered over the country—there, and there, and there. And yet it was just empty. And it was as if a hand had brushed over the marshes, everything was brushed away, there was nothing. Everything here was *marked.* It was *not real.*

Someone came out and called him. He crouched down behind the hedge.

Then he crept away towards the cowshed, looked in through the opening at the empty stalls where she used to go milking. What a nice, warm smell of milk there had been, especially on winter evenings when you came in from the cold. She used to press her forehead against the cow she was doing, and when you came in she didn't hear you with the hissing in the pail. He went behind the cowshed, out into a meadow with rowans and junipers; slunk along by the edges of it; crept around the farm and stared at the windows of the little room, where he knew that she and the rest of them were sitting.

At last it was time for them to get back to the train. Then he came and said good-bye to her like the others. Again she gave him a long look. It was as if she realized that he didn't care for her as much as they did.

He always felt it like that, only as a misery.

He remembered one time especially—Mother and he came out one day in the summer. As they came up the path they saw the old woman taking up potatoes in the garden plot; a few in a pan to have for dinner. She was on her knees on the soil, because the pain wouldn't let her bend. When she'd finished she couldn't get up; Mother and he had to help her. It was hard at first for her to stand, as if she just wanted to sink down again, and her eyes were like glass, as though she didn't see them. He shook as if he too were going to sink down, couldn't keep himself upright or support her. But Mother brushed the soil off her and helped her in.

Then he had to get away from them, stood by the end of the house and cried. That was perhaps the only time he was able to cry.

There was something inhuman in his horror of death. It was as if really he felt no pity. Everything was swallowed up in his horror at what was happening to her. He saw her before him continually, every day, from morning till night. Somehow he didn't think of *her*, only that she was going to die. Only of how dreadful it was that among them someone should be going about and dying. It was as if he didn't know who it was. When he remembered it he clung to his memory of her as she had been, when she was living, when she wasn't going to die. Now she no longer existed, you felt that she wasn't here, that she didn't belong here. You had to *remember* her.

There was something inhuman in this demented clinging to life—something deadly.

In the winter, after she'd had to take to bed, the old woman slowly dwindled away. She left them gradually, no longer saw them so clearly and couldn't quite follow when they talked to her. She couldn't follow the work on the farm either; sometimes she asked, wanted to know about this or that, but when they told her it was as if she hadn't heard. Once, one evening, she'd asked where she was. And when they told her she was in the little side room she was astonished; she'd thought the room was a lot bigger.

They wrote and told them things of this kind in the note that came with the milk. It came early every morning with a few lines from them. It was a cold winter and the note was always frozen; Mother had to breathe on it before she could unfold it without spoiling the writing.

She went out more and more often, and towards the end she stayed there. She and the old man, her father, were the ones who always kept watch by the dying woman. He sat over by the window and read out of the Bible. She looked after her, crept quietly in and out of the door, bent down to hear when she whispered what she wanted. The old man could no longer hear her. But she whispered to Mother that she could hear when he read. So he sat there all the time and went on. The snow lay in drifts high up against the windows; in other places the earth was bare and several fruit trees were killed by the frost that winter.

All the children went out there one evening to say good-bye to her, but she couldn't really distinguish them. A few days later Mother wrote with the milk that it was over.

Anders felt it almost as a relief. His brothers and sisters talked about Grandmother the whole day, what she'd been like that time and the other—often from a long time back—what she'd said that time, how early she always had to get up in the morning, what bread twists she could bake, how she looked after her flower beds, her peonies, how as a girl she'd once got lost in the woods and had to turn her jacket inside out—about everything. Anders kept joining in eagerly. He could remember, too—yes, ever so much, ever so much! He talked, he remembered—and wherever the talk went on, in the kitchen, in the living rooms, there he would be. He was glowing with eagerness and his eyes shone. . . . It was as if she were alive again.

Mother came home to sew and fit out the children for the funeral. The girls, the two boys, there was work to be done for all of them. Anders was confirmed that year; he had his black suit earlier than the other boys. He'd never worn black before. It felt queer. People looked at you, at the crêpe band around your cap. Specially when the children were all together, Mother with them perhaps, all in black—people looked at them and made way for them, greeted them in a special kind of way. You felt subdued when you had to go through the streets together. You felt different from other people.

On Sunday morning they went out to the funeral, early. Sprigs of fir had been strewn in the snow outside the gates and all up the path. The garden looked bare in the bleak weather, but indoors it was warm. Some had arrived already, mostly old people who were warming their hands at the open fire where the fir wood burned and crackled, hissed out sparks onto the floor. The floor had been freshly scrubbed and the old women kept to the rugs, whispering together and greeting newcomers, with folded handkerchiefs in one hand. When the mourners from the town arrived, Mother and Father and all the children, it grew even quieter. All the old people came up and took their hands in a slow clasp. Little or nothing was said. In the middle of the room stood a tall red-bearded man who had moved to the district not many years before and talked out loud.

More and more arrived. Sledges drew up by the cow-shed and old women bundled up in shawls got out. People came up the path the whole time, most of them old. Out on the roads you could see others who were also on their way, hobbling along, those who had to come on foot. Many like that had been asked; here at the farm, too, they had no horse and had borrowed one for the funeral. One after the other they came in, tall, thin peasant women, toothless, with sunken breasts, in black dresses that smelt of moth balls, and men from the neighbouring farms in big bulging suits. The whole house was full. There were people in the rooms upstairs as well, where the floors had been cleared of onions and apples. You could hear them moving about.

Then the door into the side room downstairs was opened and an icy draught went through the whole house. They solemnly crowded in. You could smell the scrubbed floor which hadn't been able to dry in the cold; the strewn fir sprigs smelled wet from the snow in them which had hardly melted. They all crowded forward to see her for the last time, say good-bye; old women who had always known her, whose heads shook with age; younger peasant wives who had never remembered her as different from what she looked as she lay there now, old and grey; old men who had danced with her at Harakulla when they were young; farm hands from Bolsgård and Jutargård whom Emil had had in and given coffee and spirits. Anders didn't press forward. He looked between the nearer ones, saw something of the forehead and a little thin hair; when someone moved and he saw that the mouth was gaping because the jaw had dropped, he gave a start and squeezed back behind the others till he could see nothing. But Helge, his elder brother, stood close by her the whole time. He was the child who'd loved her most, spent most time with her, and it didn't frighten him that she was dead; it was as if to him it was not bewildering. He had helped her to get up hay and to watch the cows, he had hoed turnips and cut lucerne, caught perch and roach for her in the stream, gone around the ledger lines in the mornings and come home with eels almost before she was up. He belonged here almost more than in the town, and no one resembled the family out here so much as he did. He stood crying gently and quietly because he'd loved her.

When they began to put the lid on the coffin, Anders felt that he wanted to rush up to it. They had to wait a little because Grandfather wanted to stroke her cheek first. And then they were such a long time before they got it screwed down. But when it was done he felt how dreadful it was that he alone hadn't taken a proper farewell of her. But it was too late now, and he stopped worrying, noticed that he could begin crying too, like the others.

Jacob of Skärvet, a venerable old man with snow-white hair that fell far down on his shoulders, struck up a hymn. His voice was cracked, but it didn't tremble; he had been a churchwarden for the greater part of his life and had sung over coffins as far back as they could remember. After that the coffin was carried out.

The horses stamped in front of all the sledges, chafing to be off. The men in their high hats with the pile rubbed up shook their whips at them, held them by the bit until the old people got in. The coffin was put on the first of the sledges and the farm hand from Jutargård drove it, because it was their horse. The cows were lowing in the shed, the fowls went under the shafts and pecked up oats. Now they were all ready and set off.

But Grandfather stood by the gates. He wasn't fit to go with them. He waved as long as they were in sight.

"I shan't be long after Stina," was the last thing he'd said.

The road to the church ran along by the stream which lay frozen at its edges. And the marshes were frozen, the whole countryside. The farms looked bleak, as they do in winter when the trees don't screen them in the ordinary way. They might have been deserted. And, in fact, almost all the people were at the funeral, sitting here in the long row of sledges which looked like a timber train, so heavy that it could hardly be hauled. The runners kept catching where the ground was bare and the people sat jolting on the seats, looking around them. Up at the front the farm hand was sitting on the coffin among a few flowers brought from the town.

When they could be seen from the church the bells began to ring. The little doors in the tower had been thrown open and the bells rang out over the whole countryside, the waste tracts and the scattered villages, right to the farms over in the woods. And as far as it could be heard the men raised their hats, as the custom was, and the women curtsied. In a hamlet almost at the edge of the parish an old woman was sitting by a window, with a shawl over her breast so that she could bear having it open.

She was the oldest in the parish, shrunken and doubled up—she hadn't left her cottage for many, many years, but her hair was jet black, with not a single grey hair, her brown eyes were bright. She was Father's mother. Perhaps she had Walloon blood, perhaps not—she had something foreign about her because she was darker than anyone was in the ordinary way around here. And she seemed somehow more distinguished than peasant women, although she was poorer; as a child she had been prepared for confirmation along with ladies. But now she sat there listening with the Bible in her lap and the window open to hear them ringing for old mother Stina, and when the first strokes reached her she clasped her hands and thrust her curiously small head out, so that the sparrows scattered into the air out of the corn sheaf that had been hung up for them from the window-frame.

The church stood on a little rise, quite insignificant like all the rises here. They drew up at the foot and carried the coffin up the slope. The bells were booming right overhead. Out among the graves stood pale children from the confirmation class, girls holding each others' hands and gazing motionless at the procession. It was the time when they were being prepared for confirmation here as well as in the town.

The burial service was held in the church. Anders realized that it was beginning now—the worst. When the organ began it meant that they were going to sing the most dreadful hymn, the ghastliest words he knew. He drew back shrinking in the pew and stared straight ahead. But they broke into the hymn almost ecstatically, clear children's voices from up in the choir and the whole congregation, all the old people down below, the organ boomed under the vaulting:

Towards death my path where'er I walk. . . .

Life—it was as if there were none, as if it were not needed

—what was the good of it! It was as if they were stupefied, as if they were giving themselves up to something near and precious, more certain than anything else. And the minister read:

From dust thou camest. Unto dust thou shalt return. . . .

If only it were over, if only it could be over! These long solemnities around death—it was terrible.

And then out to the grave!

All the church people came, the uninvited last. The freshly opened grave could be seen far off because the clods lay in a great heap at the side; they'd had to be raised up with crowbars, the ground was frozen three feet down. They all gathered around and then you heard her being lowered.

Still, this wasn't so bad as he'd expected. Everything that goes on out-of-doors is easier. The wind was so cold that you shivered—you could feel the chill of it. And the snow got into your overshoes. Boys he had played with stood looking at him. It wasn't so oppressive and solemn. When he threw his flowers into the grave he was able to cry.

Then they went back to the church and stayed for the ordinary service.

Afterwards they went home, the whole long row as before. There had been a sprinkling of snow, so that it was easier going even over the bare ground. The horses were allowed to set their own pace and it didn't take long. Grandfather stood on the steps to receive them, looked for the empty sledge coming behind. Mother told him about it all, what had happened, the whole funeral from beginning to end. He asked what the roads had been like; she'd forgotten to mention that.

But dinner was ready, laid on two trestle tables placed at right angles. They were loaded with food and steam came in from the kitchen when they went backwards and forwards. The old women gave sidelong glances at the table, the men chafed their hands together after the cold and waited for their drinks.

They sat down and there they were sitting right on into the evening. Dishes were carried around, one after the other, simple but many, and a lot of each. You had to have some of them all, once at least, although several were almost the same. It was a sustaining feast, not meant just for tasting. The men drank spirits with it. For the first hour they kept solemn. But later on they got talkative and called right across the table and from one end to the other, sprawled forward. They sat squeezed together so that they could hardly move. The chairs, borrowed from here, there and everywhere, were packed close. Up by the door there was only a plank to sit on and the bench that stood in the arbour in the summer. When any of the old men by the wall had to go outside they all had to make way for him; it didn't go unnoticed, and the women who never went out made good-natured protests. It grew livelier as it went on and the room and everyone in it warmed up. The open fire in the hearth burned up well in the heat. They sweated.

The sense of well-being grew. They talked. Old men who were known as wags livened up and began to feel their way with a broad grin, tried their jokes on each other. Those near by listened, the women with their heads on one side. Other men sat talking seriously, about heifers that were going to calve, chalk and hypophosphates, making drains and reclaiming bogs. But always in a loud voice, so that everyone should know what they thought about this and the other and what they thought here and now.

Apart from the farmers there was Massa-Janne, a short little tailor, born and bred in the parish. He spluttered when he talked, and he'd made all the clothes for the big fellows here. When he was measuring he stood on a foot-stool, savage because it was necessary, but getting his own back by spluttering on them all the time. And the miller, who was the only fat one at the funeral, with a backside that bulged out over the chair and between the rails at the back. Anders who was sitting beside him saw that the tuft of hair in his ear was mealy. And perched on the garden bench farthest off by the door sat Peter of Lyckan, who was a thin man and hadn't any land. He never spoke and never looked up, just hung his shaggy head over the plate. They said that he didn't eat for several days if he thought he was going to be asked out. Sometimes he made a mistake, and had to start eating again. At home he had boiled potatoes and stale bread in the table drawer, which he pushed under if anybody came. But probably the truth was just that he was poor and needed food, his own and other people's too. And they didn't really mind about it, though they sometimes chaffed him a bit. He sat farthest off by the door, partly because he was the least important and partly because it was darker there and they didn't notice how much he took.

Round about five, after all the meat, the sweets began; it was already pitch dark. Everyone's contribution had to be brought out, curd cakes, cream cheeses, abundance of every sort. They were much alike, but people recognized their own by the cloth around the copper dish and each housewife saw to it that everyone tasted hers. Nothing is more filling than that kind of thing. They straightened themselves up and grunted with satisfaction, feeling they'd well deserved it; even Peter of Lyckan heaved himself up a bit and glowered timidly a little way down the table.

It seemed fine to Anders with all the buzz and warmth, all the old men and women talking and eating and not like they were before. It felt so safe here. The fire crackled and the heat seemed to bemuse you. He sat by the wall. Behind their backs the window panes were pitch black, but here in the room there was light enough. In the middle of the trestle table stood the big paraffin lamp and the small one right at the end; down by the door there were candles, everything was lit up. But in the place of honour by the minister sat Mother, pale and still, pale somehow because of all the light. She didn't seem to be talking to anyone.

Now dinner was almost over. But last and most impressive was a cake from the town, decorated in black and white, with a great black cross in the middle. It was greatly admired; everyone had to have some. Anders shuddered when it got near him. He let it go past though he could see that he'd never had anything so good. The miller took a great bit of the cross and ate it all in one mouthful.

Then at last they got up; the minister solemnly said grace.

Doors were thrown open and they scattered. The porch was full of clothes as if a whole parish lived in the house; you could hardly get past among the piles of overcoats that smelled of hay and the cowshed. But the rooms upstairs were empty, and there it was pleasantly cool after all the heat. A faint smell lingered from the apples and onions. Behind the mirror was a bunch of lavender which Grandmother used to take a little of when she went to church. There they went for coffee, with biscuits for the women and brandy for the men. It was soon hot and full of people there, too; they gossiped and gossiped.

Anders didn't quite know what to do with himself. He was the youngest, had no one of his own age to go with. He wandered about at random for a bit, or stood against a wall somewhere. He pushed the kitchen door ajar, as he used to; there were only strange people there, clearing away and washing up, and whole heaps of china that didn't belong here at the farm—the plates had a rose in the middle. Then he went upstairs, looked into the rooms, stood still and listened. The women were sitting in one, but in the other the old men were roaring over their toddy glasses; it was thick with smoke and they were all talking at once. No one could be heard, just noise and confusion. He enjoyed it there. Still, after a while he went down again. On the wall at the side of the stairs was a crude painting showing the road from the farm to the church, the farm at the bottom and the church at the top with a few crosses and birches round it, and the road winding along by the handrail. But today he didn't look at it, hurried down, pushed open the outer door, went out onto the steps of the porch.

It was pitch dark; cold but perfectly still, no wind. Among the currant bushes a few old peasants stood relieving themselves, big and broad in the darkness; it was like the gushing from horses. To the east the stars were showing; there were clouds everywhere else. When the old men had gone he stayed there by himself in the stillness.

Down in the cowshed he could see a light shining through the little window where the cows were, but dimly, because the pane was covered with cobwebs. After a while someone came out with the milkpail in one hand and the lantern in the other. She went up the path. The light travelled over the ground and over the grey skirt that reached down to her feet. When she got near the house with its lights she turned aside down the kitchen path. He saw that she was a middle-aged stranger whom he didn't know.

Down by the stream the ice was crackling; it was freezing over. It struck him that it was cold and that he was only here to do the same as the old men. But he went over to the apple tree by the gable, because that was where he always went.

There was a hubbub of voices from the whole house. It was so crammed with people that it seemed to creak—garrulous people, not used to talking much. He stood with his back to it. But through the hubbub came a voice that seemed not to be talking to anyone, a calm and clear voice that nothing interrupted, that no one made any reply to.

He turned around. Down in the gable was a window that seemed extraordinarily quiet, just as if no one were inside. It was in the little side room—he stood looking towards it.

When he'd finished he went up and looked in. Inside sat his grandfather upright in the bed which his old wife had died in, reading out of the Bible that lay wide open on the sheep rug in front of him. He had a clean shirt on; you could see it was quite new, the linen was unbleached. And the sheets hadn't been used before; they were perfectly smooth. His white hair, freshly combed, fell down on his shoulders; every strand lay in place. He sat solemnly, as if it were a great ceremony. The sprigs of fir were still on the floor. Tall juniper bushes stood in the corners.

Anders breathed heavily against the pane so that it got misted over. He wanted to go, but he wiped the window and stayed there. The crust on the drift of snow that lay up against the wall wouldn't bear him any longer; he sank through. He could feel the stalks in the flower bed underneath the snow. Now he had to heave himself up as far as he could so as to see; the window pane was frozen at the bottom.

The old man sat motionless. Upstairs they were talking and shouting. He took no notice—perhaps didn't hear it; read in the loud voice that he had always had. The toothless mouth was moving. Anders could hear every word distinctly.

At last he shut the Bible and clasped his hands over it.

"Amen. In the name of God Almighty. Amen."

But when he had laid the book on the chair beside him, he gazed across the room and began speaking again.

"At the last day the Lord thy God shall waken thee."

Then he lay down and blew out the light, and the darkness seemed just to swallow him up.

Anders was now growing out of childhood. He began to roam about the town and far out on the roads, with friends and without, as though he didn't like being at home. He felt such a strange weight there. There was something oppressive in all that constraint, all the heaviness in his home. And in the way everything there was bound together, the people and what they had around them, everything was just one. The old furniture and the air in the rooms, the rag mats, woven in the country, and those who walked about on them—it seemed all one and the same. When you came in through the door and spoke to the people in the rooms—then it was just that you'd come home. And when they sat round the lamp after supper and his sisters crocheted and the lamplight reached halfway up the wall and you heard the trains outside—then it was just an evening at home. Father and Mother read the Bible, as they always had, serious and burdened by the words. It felt like a weight on your chest. And yet everything was peace. Everything secure and calm. Why should it be?

They were all bound together. They had everything in common; seemed to sit shut up in a room by themselves, cut off from the world; lived, all one and the same, their life which never seemed to change. . . .

They were just a family, not separate people—you had to break out of it, be a self apart!

And now he began to break out of it.

It wasn't noticed. No one could notice it. It was hard for anything in them to show itself, to come to the surface. It just buried itself, hid away so that they didn't really understand it themselves. They only felt it. It was so with everything; they cnly felt it. And now he was feeling this; groped his way through it, crouching, as if in a cellar.

What was happening was brutal, like a birth. With the same distress and anguish, anxiety for a new waking life and for an old. And in some way sickening—because something was falling to pieces, changing, almost rotting. What was it that was changing? Why was it changing?

Animals drag themselves away when they're going to bear young, into their holes, into the darkness, howl where no one can hear them and moan as they bite through the navel string. And the blind litter sniffs at the blood the earth sucks up. . . .

Belonging to a family—why should you?

He felt the pain of what was going on within him. And yet he carefully probed each little change, to make sure of keeping up with it all the time. He seemed almost to relish it. . . .

For the first time he felt what incoherence and cheating there is in living. How half-heartedly and insincerely you can live, and still manage. Life itself forces you into it and sees to it that you get on. Every foothold slips away from you—you still keep going. For the first time he wasn't living in the middle of himself. He always had done so until now.

It was the beginning of youth, the most wretched age of man. And rightly, because it is the falsest, most unreliable, most worthless. Those who haven't discovered this have been so false that they have deceived even themselves. Childhood, manhood, age, they can all be meaningful and real for us. Youth is something unworthy of men. A rootlessness, an irresponsible freedom of personality, a fertilizing disintegration, insincerity, falsity, in life itself—but unworthy of men. No doubt that's why all the hollow phrase-mongers shout about it; they got on best then. It was their time. It was then that the least was required of them and the most offered. But he was still only at the beginning.

He edged away from their God, stole away without being noticed. Before long he was standing outside in the darkness and all around him was empty space. He shuddered—almost with pleasure. He felt how it *is*, really *is*—

just empty. Yes, it was empty, *he* knew that. He'd known that a long time, as long as he could remember. So it was better really to feel it, to stand right out in the darkness—it was easier that way. A great destiny to support.

If he could only stay there in the emptiness, only exist there. There would be nothing to lament in that fate, it would suit him well. In the darkness—he would do well there.

But he was going to die. Soon. They all knew it. They did know it, of course. It was the lung trouble he'd got; he was going to die of that. People always kept a few paces away from him so that he shouldn't infect them. His brothers and sisters, too, though they disguised it a bit more, didn't want him to notice it too obviously. That wounded you just the same—in fact worse. They could have saved themselves that! He would have liked to shout it in their faces.

That they always kept about two steps away from him—wasn't it obvious enough? Could there be any doubt about it? Hadn't he eyes? Didn't he observe it all, every look, every tone, every little word, even those they whispered in the kitchen, in the little room, where they shut themselves in—they shut the door between the rooms, it had never been shut before? Didn't he realize that they'd already begun to mourn for him? Didn't he feel their oppression, a gloomy distress in the house—the horror of someone walking about among them and dying? He saw it all; he understood it all. It was clear enough. . . .

Only his mother showed nothing, didn't mind how near she came. But then she stood above and beyond both illness and death, beyond everything, wasn't part of this. She was so good. She was afraid that he should notice anything at all. Things must be as usual, he mustn't be allowed to guess anything, only feel how much he was loved, especially now, how they thought of him—she went about constantly thinking of him, of his illness; she always wanted to be near him, as if no one could say how long. . . . She betrayed herself more than anyone else.

This spring he had an egg for lunch when he came in from school, something the others didn't have; she said he needed it. Every day it was waiting there as a reminder—in case he might have forgotten. And she took the chair next to him and talked—after all there were plenty more chairs around the kitchen table; there were only the two of them at home at his lunchtime, she didn't need to sit just there. She talked about everything except what they were both thinking of, talked as if to prevent him from getting worked up, so gently that it hurt him—never a reproach, never a hard word, although he'd stopped going to church, although he'd stopped saying grace. She forgave it all, took no notice. . . . He couldn't bear her tenderness. If only he could have hated her!

All that kindness, all that affection there was at home—you couldn't bear it. Never a raw gust of wind to sweep in. You sat shut in, protected, comfortable, in a peace that bound them together but didn't liberate them, didn't help them. There was a dull heat inside them that never burst into flame but just gave out warmth, warmth; nothing ran to waste, there was no fire to be seen. . . . Perhaps that was why it troubled and oppressed him so much, because it never burst into flame, never burned up! They only had it to warm themselves by. And his parents' fear of God, heavy and primitive, a primeval calm that they tried to feel—while they sighed, just sighed. It pressed down and down, as if it wanted to smother you. . . . You had to break out of it!

No, the new doctrine that you picked up, which swept away God and all expectation, which laid life open and raw in all its nakedness, all its systematic meaninglessness, that was better, that helped. And it was true, too. No faith—just things as they are.

Nothing made any difference to him, he who was only

going to die. But all the same he must break out of it. Out where it was colder, raw—so that you could breathe for the little while you had left.

Yes, it was good to know that it was empty. It prepared you for what was coming. You could perhaps get used to the emptiness, so that you didn't think of it as so dreadful and need not live so feverishly, anguished for the little while. . . .

No, he could never get used to it. But he soaked up the doctrine, greedily, revelled in it. It seemed to be made for him. It helped him, hardened his heart. And it explained his childhood, all the desolation and anguish that had been lying in wait in the surrounding darkness, in spite of the security of his home, in spite of all he had possessed there. . . . What he felt had been right. Now he felt it even more, and it was still more right.

It didn't make him calm or happy, but it had to be. Everything was slipping away; there was no firm ground—he was slipping with it. Nothing was certain, nothing stood fast—you could believe anything before long. Only the emptiness stood all around unchanging. Only the anguish gnawed and gnawed, eating a hole in you—you could feel it in your breast, the hole grew bigger and bigger. . . .

When he was weary and thought how he was only going to die, he felt like giving up. To break away, what use was that? Better to sink into peace in the security of home, where it was all so certain, and Mother would sit holding his hand, and read to him out of the hymn book, as she would so gladly, as he knew she would so gladly. . . .

No. It wouldn't do. You'd got to have the truth. Just as it *was*. Even if you were only going to die, you'd got to live life just as it is—at home it was stifling with all the security and peace. You'd got to break out of it!

He realized that. He was doing it. . . .

He felt almost hunted. . . . And his body was often so hot, as if it were burning. . . . Very likely it was the illness, the fever—or the instincts that were waking, that had lain hidden in the child and now broke out, dull and unconscious, more and more suffocating. . . . Perhaps they were the hunters. He didn't know. No one knew. You scudded on, not knowing where—with only the beginnings of brutality as a helpless defence, an attempt to understand what it was all about and conceal all one's uncertainty and longing from others and from oneself.

But he was going to die. It all meant nothing to him, he was only going to die; walked about waiting—nothing more. He seemed to be standing outside. Like someone listening by a door. . . .

That was how he felt. That was how things were for him.

But life is mercifully confused, not simply one. Least of all for him, who was constantly swinging from one thing to another.

As a matter of fact he was mostly bright and cheerful. No one could notice anything else, not even he himself often.

The least little thing could make his heart leap with zest. Just that it was sunny for a moment. Or a shower of rain if there'd been sun for a long while. Or nothing at all—just that it hadn't changed for a long while, that it stayed as it was. Anything at all. As soon as he came up from his cellar the world lay strangely open to him. Then there was nothing wrong, not a cloud in sight. And at those times all that was good and orderly in it was real and tangible. Yes, if he wanted he need only stick his head out through the opening. . . .

This life that he had inside himself mingled with a variety of other experiences, one thing and another. In the winter, for example, when they went skating, nearly all day—slipped away across the lakes that lay everywhere. Where one ended the next began. They walked on the point of the skates over the strip of land, struck out across the next. If the school was shut for cleaning, they could set out early; when there was morning frost and the ice rang. Old men stood fishing through holes in the ice far out, looked like small dots. If you came up to them they didn't say a word, just glared. You pretended not to notice, did a silent figure eight and then shot off again. You easily got right away to the signalman's house at Näs, flew around the point and scared the fowls with wild outside edges, so that they tore away to the house panic-stricken. Here as in many places there was a current underneath, because a stream ran out at that point. You had to keep an eye open for those; there were sometimes branches to mark them, sometimes not. There were big and little islands that you could skate around in that lake. And on the north-east shore there were the bathing places. They looked funny now it was winter; you could hardly recognize the bush that you undressed by.

Then in the evening they got together a heap of reeds and made a fire, came charging along with great armfuls from the creeks, right up to the fire, swung aside just in time and flung them in. The flames shot up, right into the sky; flakes of ash swirled around in eddies. The ice melted, crackling because of the heat and because there were too many of them standing round. It split and roared far out into the darkness.

They came home starving, their faces red, to dry their skates at the fire. Their toe nails were ingrown, and they had to have warmed-up food; dinner and supper were both over long ago.

It was a fine life. Nothing wrong with it. It wasn't like his. But wasn't he in this, too, really?

Yes, he had different kinds of life, two at least. And he felt almost as if they had nothing to do with each other. He could break off completely, be as lively as anything. . . . But the cheerful vigour would break off suddenly as well.

Anyhow he got on fine living like that, different kinds of

life. It was exciting. And so it need be when your time was so short.

That illness now, what was it really? When he wasn't actually thinking about it, it gave him no trouble at all. Yes, you'd got to be carefree a bit, let things take their own course. That's what they would do anyhow.

He had friends, hung about with them. There was one called Jonas, a good fellow. He was from the country; he was studying for something. In the wintertime they had profound talks with one another; in the summer they snared pike. He had a wooden arm. He'd had his right arm cut off in a threshing machine when he was a child. But he was handier than anyone, could do everything with just his left hand and do it better than most. He was specially good at snaring pike, and they spent a lot of time at that in the summer when Anders was staying with him at his home, some miles out from the town. There were lakes there, too—several. One with low muddy grass edges was specially good; you crept right out to the edge where the pike lay asleep in the blazing sun. You had to take off your shoes higher up on the edge of the wood a long way from the lake. Even then it wasn't easy to move quietly and it got harder and harder because of the squelching. Jonas always went first. That was only right; he was the one who could catch them. Anders came behind. He got the tag end of it. If he squelched too much, Jonas shook his one good fist at him and a deathly quiet fell. He was incredible; crouched down and crept along the edge, saw the pike a long way off where they dozed under the water lily leaves; made a noose in the gut, drew it over their heads, and so it was done. It wasn't long before they had a whole row spiked on a crotched stick. He was the plague of the people who thought they owned the fishing, those who couldn't catch anything.

It didn't follow that Jonas came home with a lot. He was just as glad to give them away going home. Sometimes there wasn't a fin left, and his mother grumbled when they arrived crestfallen at the cottage; afterwards she'd get them coffee and cakes.

The village where they lived was strangely desolate—so Anders thought at least—but perhaps it was because he was a stranger. The houses were all unpainted and not too well kept. Often only three or four of the windows had curtains. It wasn't well looked after outside either—no gardens, just the bare earth with the well and perhaps an apple tree. Whether that was the reason or not, there was a curiously empty and unfriendly look between the houses, although they were so close together. It looked as though people never called on one another, didn't really know each other. But Jonas knew them all, greeted them cheerfully—girls who were drawing water, farm hands who were carting dung or hay. And you could tell they were used to shaking hands with him—it couldn't have come easy at first, because he used the left.

There were big woods around the village. And he went shooting as well. He was notorious for that, too. Brought up his gun with a jerk and had the aim at once, as he had to if he were to hold it still. Shot hares and ducks, woodcocks, anything there was. And in the autumn grouse by torchlight, which was forbidden but customary in that part. He was handy at everything.

They had a good time in the country. It was different, of course, in the winter in town. Then they had to spruce themselves up. Their conversations became more solemn and more enlightened in every way when they went for a walk in the most distinguished of the streets. But they forgot themselves sometimes, slouched along as if they were on a country road. Jonas was by nature remarkably carefree in the way he walked. It was as thought nothing mattered very much. Every now and again he pulled at his wooden arm up by the shoulder to see that it was still there all right. At those times his face was always lit up by a good-natured grin.

Here in town he tended to be a bit vain. The glove on the artificial hand always had to be correct. The moment it was worn and the wood stuck through he bought a new one. One specially lovely spring when he began to go with a girl he got himself a light grey one and was more elegant than ever.

But he was superb. He had a roguish half-smile that would have taken him far if he'd bothered about it. But he'd already seen through the world, discovered pretty well what it was like and soon went back to his village—he'd just as soon live there.

Then there was another called Murre, small, no bigger than a midget. Anders had known him right from his first school; after that Murre had left and gone to be a cycle repairer. They only met on Sundays now when he was free. If they ran across each other in the street on a weekday his hands were greasy and he wouldn't shake hands with more than his thumb. But every Sunday he came along in a stiff turn-down collar like a gentleman, and they went out for a walk together, puffing at penny cigars that Murre was able to provide for them by his work.

Generally they followed the railway line out into the woods and then walked about the roads there. They'd played there as boys, knew every bit of it. They liked to talk of that time as something long past, smiling indulgently when they found that they could still recall this and the other from that time. But if they went past the stone that Anders had out there, he walked along looking in the other direction and talked eagerly all the time. They didn't possess that in common; the other knew nothing about it.

He had these and several more. One who never talked sense, whose good sense consisted in that. One who lived in beauty, none of the others knew what it was. And with all of them their talk was deep and considered.

But there was a lot that you could never talk about to anyone. All that you were really thinking about. Or what you just had in you, what weighed on you.

After having parted towards evening from his Sunday friend, the cycle repairer, he often had to go out to the stone again. He was tired by then, and in other ways, too, it was no pleasure to him. He just went all the same.

On the way he tried to think what it was like when they'd been there just a little before—that it was exactly the same now, of course. It hadn't got dark yet; there was still almost as much light. He thought of lots more things that went on from day to day, that he thoroughly enjoyed; there were plenty of those. And how he was bound up with them, really belonged among them. Yes, didn't he take ever so much more pleasure in everything than most of the others? Couldn't he be overflowing with it, sometimes at least, with everything around him, with a joy that came from he didn't know where? Yes, that's how it was.

Living in this way, having his being and looking around him, as he was on the embankment now this evening, wasn't he really quite happy? Just as happy as the rest. Yes—so he was. Exactly like the rest.

What he himself had to put up with specially, that was just something he imagined. That was of no account.

That he had come out here, for instance. That had nothing to do with him, with anything that he was. Not now. As a child he had been driven by an inner need, lain here in deep and possessing faith, as if in ecstasy. Later he had gone on with it with a sense of working through its stages. In the end it had become just an empty convention.

By now it was hardly that even. Had no meaning. He just did come out here.

Now he was standing there; came and stood on the same spot as always; you could see the mark in the grass. He didn't fall on his knees, hadn't for many years. But he clasped his hands as hard as he could, so hard that he seemed to feel it in his whole body, really *feel* that he was clasping his hands. With that he reached a sort of numbness. Then he prayed.

But only that he might live. Nothing else. Just as before, just as always. Just to live—nothing beyond that. Then everything could go as it would. So long as he didn't die.

He didn't think of any God. Hadn't any faith. And not a thought of its helping him in any way, giving him an inner strength, having any sort of meaning in it. It meant nothing.

What he prayed for—that didn't matter either. But there had to be something. And so it was always that, always the same.

No, it meant nothing. It was just a compulsion; he realized himself that it only came from being overwrought.

He was free. He had broken out of it.

One autumn night Anders was on his way through the town. He was going up to the north part, almost on the outskirts. It was overcast and getting dark; it had been raining a little while before. The streets were wet, shone wherever there was a street lamp, only every other one was alight. It was deserted, no one about, only a policeman on the corner by the square. There were lights there in the windows, but the blinds were drawn; they were playing a piano in one house. He kept on past them. Walked quickly, with his collar turned up.

When he came to Norrgatan he turned through a gateway, into a courtyard. It was almost pitch black there, difficult to see; there were carts standing about and heaps of old iron, a jumble of old scrapped wheels and rusty iron plates. Farthest in was a small, low house with a light burning, but the windows lay in the other direction. You could hear singing from inside, but faintly as if the walls were very thick. Still the singing was enough to guide him so that he found the entrance. He opened the door and went in.

It was a gloomy, whitewashed room, small windows, the roof like a vault. In the middle a massive pillar that you could see wasn't meant as a support; it blocked the view so that you couldn't see the whole room. Old women were sitting huddled up on unpainted benches, a few young men with their caps on their knees, young women, a few boys behind the pillar. Up at the front was a platform with two paraffin lamps hanging down from the roof. Sitting there in the light were Salvationists; up against the wall, by the rail at the front, stood two women, officers, singing to the guitar. He went and sat down on a bench.

There was heating, but the room wasn't warm. They all kept their coats on. They sat on benches, huddled together in the body of the hall where it was almost dark; the front benches stood empty. Nearest the door sat mad Johan from the workhouse, alone, his head thrust forward and his eyes shining in the darkness. The walls glistened with water; they were sooty where the whitewash had flaked off. It was an old disused smithy, which had been rented to them. The forge had been in the middle; it was bricked in.

They sang—clearly and rather shrill, but still with feeling; it was mostly women. The guitars twanged. The singing sounded shut in, as if it were a cellar. You could hear the two officers' voices above all the others, truer and better trained. They stood in the middle of the light, with upturned faces, burning eyes, ecstatic, never looked down at the book like the others, knew it by heart. They had their coats on, buttoned up to the throat. One was dark and full-blooded, with something restrainedly sensual in her shining eyes and about her mouth when she parted her big warm lips. The other was slight, almost like a child. Her delicate form seemed to draw no strength from itself, but stood there surrendered to the light. There was something pathetic about her, something at the same time helpless and courageous. Her face was pale, the features poor, like a peasant girl's; they weren't delicate perhaps, but they had a sensitiveness that was much more beautiful. Her eyes were not bright; there was just a quiet light within them. Her hair showed under the bonnet, lay pale and delicate on her cheeks, seemed almost without colour. And burning like fire—like a flame, fed with wax.

Anders looked at her the whole time. He knew her.

They were working up; sang more fervently, as if to fan the embers within them into a flame. At first you felt that it was deliberate. Then it began to burst forth of itself. They were carried away, seemed to be tranced. Someone began to testify. And the others murmured after him. "Thanks be to Jesus. Praise be, glory to Thee! Hallelujah! Praise and glory." They sighed and prayed with their faces in their hands. One woman sat rocking to and fro. The soldier who was testifying was wrought up by them, spoke more vehemently, stood with his eyes shut, the words poured out of his mouth. He stood as if in a trance. And the others were carried with him; it was as though a wave lifted them, rose and fell, carried them all with it. Someone down in the hall began to groan. Right back in the darkness mad Johan sat gaping with fevered eyes.

Anders felt more and more uncomfortable. It almost sickened him. It was stifling, you could scarcely breathe....

They gabbled on. They didn't even talk about God, but just of Jesus and again Jesus; that was something specially repugnant to him, that part of the faith that had first repelled him, become most foreign to him. They sighed and rejoiced about that alone. The whole air hung heavy, it weighed on your chest, you gasped, couldn't get your breath. . . . It was something worked up, overwrought—nothing for him.

She was going to testify now, the young Salvation officer whom he knew. She went up to the rail and began to speak without looking up. You could see that she was uncertain, not quite used to being an officer yet. But there was light about her. She told how she'd been saved, how Jesus had come to her. Thanks be! Praise and Glory! How he took her out of her sin and grief and gave her a new life. It was so much better now. She didn't fret about anything now, as the children of the world do. All her troubles she laid on him. She said it so simply that there was nothing miraculous left in it. And yet she seemed to shine.

Anders sat is quiet wonder, motionless, his eyes fixed on her. The boys tittered behind the pillar. He started as if he'd wakened up. But he forced himself not to hear, to notice nothing but her.

She gained courage. Now and again she raised her eyes, looked up into the hall. But the mumble of prayer on all sides didn't work upon her; when they sighed and groaned her voice only grew warner in some way. There was something clean and poor about her as she stood there in her coat of dark blue serge. It was worn. It was quite shiny in some places, especially on the left side, where she used to carry the bundle of papers when she was out selling *The War Cry*. But he liked the look of the worn places here in the lamplight. It was as if there were light on the cloth. It suited her. Anders thought so anyhow. He never took his eyes off her, off her face, which grew more exposed as she talked, as if you were seeing her for the first time now. The pale mouth seemed to smile when she opened it. But it wasn't a smile, only something sensitive and good in the lips themselves. It just *was*.

When she stopped they began to pray with the unconverted down in the hall; kneeled by the benches, praying. The soldiers up on the platform sang meanwhile, worked up feeling. The guitars twanged. You could hear the groaning through it all. In the gloom you could see hardly anything, just that some of them were bowed over the benches. It was they who groaned.

The praying grew more fervid. It went on and on. All

who were saved prayed; gabbled on, burning. "Oh Jesus, our Saviour! Look upon the sinner, Oh let him find you! Oh let him find you now, now tonight! Oh save a soul tonight! Oh, before we part, let a soul be saved. Oh, then shall we sing and praise thee! Oh Jesus! Oh let this meeting not have been in vain! Oh open the gates of heaven for a sinner tonight!"

They went on and on. The whole room had grown hot, the air felt heavy, unendurable. . . .

Anders sat pale, tense, his eyes feverish—he gasped, his breast was heaving violently. . . . It seemed as though he was going to begin groaning with them! Begin screaming! He wanted to. . . .

He clung to the bench. . . .

A little way in front a young Salvation officer was praying with a working woman. He caught a glimpse of her face; saw that she was perfectly calm. She wasn't worked up like him. Why wasn't she?

Quietly, with clasped hands, she knelt and whispered. Perhaps she was praying—perhaps only talking—you couldn't hear. Her lips moved, but it couldn't be for vehement words, you could see that. Everything about her was simple and ordinary. Her shoes stuck out from the bench, her skirt was a little crumpled. Only the red band round the bonnet flamed above her.

They implored and prayed; sang and sang—the same, always the same. They groaned in the benches, sighed, wrestled. They sweated the soul out of themselves, the whole room felt full up—the vaulted roof pressed down, the walls squeezed together, you were cooped in, couldn't escape.

At last one of them dragged himself to the front, a young man, tottered as if asleep, up into the light, clung to the rail, cried out that he was saved. His face was washed out, empty, expressionless, he just looked dazed. Then he began gabbling, the words poured out of him. . . . They rejoiced and sang! The guitars twanged. Thanks be! Praise be to thee! Thanks be to Jesus! They took up the collection; sang once more. Thanks be to Jesus! Praise be to thee.

At last it was over. Anders hurried out. Across the yard, out into the street, the first to come out.

He turned up his collar, walked up and down. He was waiting for her.

What he felt was nausea. Complete loathing. And icy cold within him, violent resentment against anything that might threaten to touch him. . . . They crowded out from the meeting, old women, ugly young women with shuffling feet, boys who ran about grinning, mad Johan and the man who'd been saved. . . . He found them revolting. Slipped over to the other side so as not to be seen, felt ashamed to be waiting.

When the street was empty she came. In her uniform—why should she go about dressed like that?

They went out of the town, made for the road to the east where they always walked. It was finer now. In some places the sky was clear, and when they got out into the country the moon came out.

He could see her. Her face showed distinctly.

He asked her how on earth she could have thought of joining the Army. She told him. There were so many at home, seven children, and she was the eldest. There wasn't enough to go around and she had to go into service. But she wasn't strong, and you've got to be if you're to work for other people. There were times when she had to give up simply from tiredness. But then she'd been saved, and there'd been no trouble of that sort since then. . . .

Did she believe? Yes, of course, she believed. Jesus had taken her to him. That evening, she'd never forget it! Yes, she was saved, she knew it. And there's nothing so wonderful as to know that. But it was good to know that she was secure too, well provided for, had food, and they got clothes in the Army, too. And if there was anything special they needed they could apply for it, and they generally got it. Yes, she was much better off now than ever before. She had put her life in God's hands. But she'd have liked to be at home with Mother and the children if she'd been allowed, if she'd been able to support herself there.

Anders listened. Her bonnet hid her face when they went along side by side. But her voice was she, too. . . . Yes. That was the way she explained it.

She said it all so simply and quietly. How could she?

They came nearer to the lake. Crossed the narrow-gauge railway that ran along by the edge. There were no trains here so late, it seemed deserted, as it does by a level-crossing when you just see the line disappearing away in both directions. But a signalman was getting back home in the darkness; you could hear the trolley farther and farther off in the woods.

The road grew muddy near the lake, her overshoe got stuck. They had to walk on the grass at the side, close to one another. He felt the warmth from her, and her breathing—and her slight hand in his. They went in silence for a long while. . . . Supposing he loved her?

Some carts were coming toward them, a whole row. The horses were worn out, their heads hanging, the men sat as if they were asleep. It was men bringing herring from the coast, sixty miles away; it was market day tomorrow. With their food and their bottle of spirits beside them they were asleep on top of the herring, which glistened in the moonlight behind their backs.

It was late. They'd have to turn back here. But they stood for a while looking at the lake. Now for a moment the moon came fully out. And the light fell right on her. Her face was revealed, her whole form. Again there seemed to be light about her, and the worn cloth in her coat seemed to be made of light, just as it was earlier in there. Wherever there was light she seemed to be revealed.

He stood watching—as if he loved her. But there was

something completely pure about her. Her features were bleached, almost unearthly—but without being transformed into ecstasy, or overwrought passion, or rapture. They were just quiet.

It was as if there were no animal in her! Why hadn't she any?

He felt suddenly as if there were something oppressive in her very purity, her goodness, even in the light there was around her. He felt that he recognized it. She seemed to resemble something he had met. . . .

There was something in some people which was terrifying because it suggested perfection, because it seemed to be wanting to imply a certainty, a perfect peace. When you met that, then everything was laid waste even more. It gave life a sudden warmth which really it didn't possess and which only made it much harder, much heavier to live.

Had they been standing here long? They must get home.

They hurried back into the town. He felt that he wanted to escape from her, or begin to talk blasphemously of what she believed in, tear down something she had. But they went along in silence.

The streets were deserted. He saw her to the smithy. There was a bit built onto it at the back, a hovel where she lived. It revolted him to stand here again by the wall that they'd been bawling and screaming behind. They parted. She went into the house as if it had been a human dwelling.

Set free from something he started on his way home.

So ended his early youth, in nothing but dissolution, falsity, confusion.

The Executioner

THE executioner sat drinking at a dimly-lit table in the inn. In the light of the single smoky candle which the innkeeper provided he leaned over the table, large and powerful in his blood-red uniform, his hand holding his forehead where the executioner's mark was branded. A few local craftsmen and some tipsy labourers were chattering noisily over their drinks further along the table, but nobody sat near him. The servant-girl crept stealthily and noiselessly across the stone floor, and her hand shook as she topped up his tankard. An apprentice who had slipped quietly in and was hanging back in the darkness held him in a long, wide-eyed stare.

"Ale's good tonight, master!" shouted one of the workmen. "S'pose you know ma's been down the gallows and pinched a finger off one o' your thieves to dip in the barrel? She'll do anything to give her customers the best ale in town, will ma: nothing like a hanged man's finger for giving it a bit of flavour, you know."

"Mm, there's all sorts of queer things come from that quarter," said a little old shoemaker with a crooked mouth, thoughtfully wiping ale from his old, lifeless beard. "There's an awful lot of power there, that there is."

"You can say that again. I remember I watched once when they were hanging a peasant down my way for poaching, though he swore he hadn't done it; well, when our friend over there knocked him off the steps and the noose tightened, he let out a fart that stank for miles around, and the flowers drooped and the east meadow—'cause the wind was to the east at the time—was all withered and eaten away, and we had no crop to speak of that summer."

The table shook with their laughter.

"Well, my father told me when he was young there was a tanner who was knocking off his sister-in-law, and he did just the same thing when they got his head in the noose—and who can blame him when it's goodbye to everything just like that—and when they stepped back for air they saw a cloud going up in the sky, a horrible sight it was, black as pitch, and there was Old Nick himself sitting in the stern alongside the tanner's wicked soul and steering with a poker, looking down at the stench with a satisfied grin on his face!"

"That's enough of your stupid nonsense," said the old man, looking askance at the executioner. "When I say there's power in evil I mean it—real power, and that's for sure. Look at Anna's boy Kristen, him who was possessed by the devil and used to fall down and start foaming at the mouth; I saw it myself lots of times and helped hold him and force his mouth open: terrible state he used to be in, I've never seen a case like it. But when Jerker the blacksmith died and Anna made Kristen take a drink of his blood, he was right as rain. He hasn't had a single tumble since that day."

"Now just a minute. . . ."

"You know that as well as I do as lives next door to 'em."

"No one can argue with that, now."

"No, it's known far and wide, is that."

"But it's got to be a murderer's blood and it's got to be warm, or it's no use."

"Right enough."

"Mm, funny thing, that. . . ."

"And like little kids what's born sick and in awful pain—they can be cured just like that if you give them blood off the executioner's sword: I've known that since I was a kid myself," said the old man. "Everyone hereabouts knew it and the midwife used to go to the hangman's house to get some: right or wrong, master?"

The executioner made no move to look at him. His large, tensed face in the shadow of his hand could scarcely be seen in the flickering candlelight.

"Yes, there's no doubt about it, evil can do wonders with healing," continued the old man.

"And what some folk'll do to get their hands on it! When I go past the scaffold on my way home at night there's a rustling and bustling there enough to scare you to death. That's where your apothecaries and your sorcerers and the rest of your godless brethren get their devilry from, so's they can sell it to the poor and hard-done-by for the little money they've had to sweat for. They say there's bodies there as have had the flesh stripped off their very bones: you'd never know they'd once been men and women. Oh, I know as well as you do that there's power there and that it's the only way when you're in real trouble: I've tried it myself if you must know—and on my own wife, too. But ugh! It's a filthy business. It's not only pigs and vultures that live on the dead: it's the likes of you and me too."

"Oh shut up will you. Listening to you just makes things worse. What was it you said you tried?"

"I didn't say, and I'm not going to either. But I want no truck with the devil—and you can take it from me, he's got a hand in everything that comes from *that* quarter."

"Aah, come off it, you're talking a lot of shit tonight. I've had enough of it."

"Why don't you drink up?"

"I *am* drinking—drink up yourself, you old soak."

"But don't you think it's funny the way it can help people, that it's got that . . . that power?"

"It's got that right enough."

"Yes, it can put pay to you either the one way or the other. When you get near it anything can happen."

They fell silent and pushed their tankards this way and that, fidgeting on the bench. Some turned away and crossed themselves gravely.

"I don't know how much truth there is in it," said the old man as he glanced across at the tall, silent figure, "but they say the hangman's proof against any weapon."

"Pack of lies!"

"Oh, some of 'em are hard cases right enough. I heard about one of 'em when I was a lad, and he was tough all right. They were going to put him to the sword for his godless ways, but the sword wouldn't go through him; so they tried the axe, but it just flew out of the axeman's hands, and then they got so scared they just let him go: they could see he had magic powers."

"Come off it!"

"It's as true as I'm sitting here."

"A load of rubbish. We all know their lordships have been finished off with swords and axes just like anyone else: look at old Jens, who was done with his own axe."

"Yeah, but Jens was another kettle of fish altogether, he wasn't really in the trade. Poor bloke, he got into trouble through no fault of his own, and had to do the job to beg a living, 'cause he couldn't bear to be parted from his wife and kids. He wasn't like the others, he couldn't stand the job. He was more scared even than the poor devil what was going to be done in. He was *afraid* of evil, he was. It was just because he was so bloody scared and never knew if he was on his head or his heels that he ended up like he did, if you ask me: that's why he did Steffan in, his best friend too. I tell you, his axe was much stronger than what he was: it kind of made him take it up, he couldn't stop himself, and one fine day it was his turn—and he knew it had to come."

"No, he didn't have any of the hangman's power; but them as have are safe against any weapon you like."

"Of course the hangman's got powers others haven't: he's

always so close to evil. And the axe and the rest of the gear's got its power too, that's for sure: that's why no one dares touch the stuff—or anything else the hangman and his kind have had their hands on."

"You're right there."

"There's powers there as no mortal can fathom, that there is. And once evil's got you, it never lets go of you."

"Don't you be so sure of that," said a man who had been sitting listening in silence the whole time. "Evil's not an easy thing to understand, but if you do get to know it you can be very surprised. I'm not saying I understand it any more than you, but well, let me put it this way: I've been where it comes from, and I've been face to face with it; I've been introduced to it, if you like. And when you've been through that, you remember it as long as you live. And the funniest thing about it is that when it's happened you're not really afraid any more."

"Go on!"

"Do you mean that? I'm not so sure."

"I'll tell you why I'm not afraid, if you're interested. While you've been sitting here chattering I've been having a think about something.

"It all happened when I was a child, about five or six years old I suppose. We lived on my father's little farm: we got a good living from it and didn't want for anything. I was the only child and they were very fond of me, too fond like as not, like most folk who've only got the one. I was happy at home and my parents—both dead now, God rest their souls—were the best and most loving you could ever hope to find. The farm was a bit off the beaten track, and I used to go for walks around there, by myself mostly, or with mother and father. I can still remember the house and the fields and the hillside and the herb-patch by the south wall, and though there's nothing left of it all now and I'll never see it again, I've still sort of got the feel of it inside me.

"But one day in the summer I was all alone at home: everyone was out at haymaking on the common and my mother had gone there to take father his food, and it was too far for her to take me along. It was a hot day with the sun blazing down and the flies buzzing around by the front door and on the hill down below the cowshed, where we'd been straining milk that morning. I wandered around looking at this and that, went into the orchard and the woods and had a quick look at the bees crawling over their hive, lazy and contented in the heat. Well, I don't know why—I suppose I must have been feeling bored or something—but I climbed over the stile and started walking along a path that led into the woods and that I hadn't ever walked very far along before. This time I went so far I got lost. Then the path went downhill and the woods became wild and dense and you looked down and saw more trees and big stones that had come away from the hillside and were overgrown with moss. Then it went up again towards the valley and you could hear the rushing of the river that flowed through the district. I enjoyed walking about there, and the summer's day and everything made me feel at peace with the world. The sun was resting peacefully in the tree-tops, the birds were singing and the woodpeckers pecking, and the smell of pine-resin hung heavy and warm in the air.

"I don't know how far I'd walked when I heard a rustling noise somewhere in front of me and saw something move behind a thicket. I hurried along to see what it was. I saw a figure running round a bend and I ran after it. The ground levelled out a bit and the wood opened into a clearing, where I saw two children running. They must have been about my age, but they weren't dressed like me. They stopped at the other side of the clearing and looked round, then took to their heels again. I chased after them and said to myself, 'I'll catch you', but they ran off the path and I kept losing sight of them in the undergrowth.

At first I thought they were playing hide-and-seek with me, but then I realized they weren't; but I wanted to catch up with them so that I could play with them for a while, and I put on a spurt and started gaining on them. In the end they separated and I saw one of them crawl under a fallen spruce so that I shouldn't see him. I rushed up to him and saw him lying hunched up among the branches. I threw myself on him, laughing and covered in sweat, and grabbed him. As he tried to break away he turned his head: his eyes were wild and terrified and his mouth twisted in an evil grin. He had short red hair and his face was covered in dirty little blotches. He had next to nothing on—only a tattered woollen smock—and he lay there scowling: it was like holding down a wild animal.

"I thought he looked a bit queer of course, but there didn't seem to be anything at all unpleasant about him, and I didn't let him go. When he tried to get up again I pinned him down with my knee and laughed at him and told him he couldn't get away.

"He didn't say anything: just lay there looking at me. But it wasn't long before I saw we'd become friends and he didn't want to run away any more. So I let go of him and we got up together and walked along side by side, but I noticed he didn't take his eyes off me for a second. The other child—it turned out to be his sister—came out from where she was hiding. He took her aside and whispered something to her and she listened with her eyes wide open in her pale, frightened little face. But when I went up to them they didn't run away.

"After a while we got round to playing together, and they enjoyed themselves. They knew about all sorts of little places they could hide in, and when I found them they'd just jump out of one and into another, without making a sound. The ground there was fairly flat, but there were big stones all over, and trees that had fallen down where they stood. Those kids knew every nook and cranny, and sometimes I hadn't a clue *where* they were, because I just couldn't hear them. I've never known kids play so quiet. They had plenty of energy, the pair of them, and they'd dart here and there like a couple of young lizards; but they hardly made a sound. And they didn't say a word to me either. Sometimes they'd stop playing and just stand there side by side looking at me, but I always thought we had fun together all the same.

"This had been going on for quite some time when one day I heard someone calling out in the woods; then they glanced at each other and they were off like a shot. I shouted out and told them I'd see them next day, but they didn't turn round and I just heard their feet running away down the path.

"When I got back home there was no one there, and when mother came back a bit later I didn't say anything about where I'd been and what I'd been doing. I don't know why, but it was . . . well, it was a sort of secret.

"Next day she went out as usual to take the haymakers their food, and as soon as I was alone I went out to find my friends. They were just as shy as before—to begin with, anyway—and I couldn't see if they were glad I'd come or not. But they were waiting there at the usual time, like they were expecting me. We started playing and the sweat was soon pouring off us from all the running and jumping. But we played in complete silence: normally I'd have been yelling and screaming for all I was worth, but they didn't, so I didn't either. I felt somehow like we'd always known each other. That day we came to a clearing in the woods, and I saw a little house close up against an overhanging rock: we didn't get very close to it, but it looked grey and a bit gloomy.

"When I got back mother was already home, and she asked me where I'd been. I told her I'd just been out in the woods for a bit.

"Then I took to going there every day. Everyone at home was so busy with the haymaking that I was left to myself and it was easy to slip away. And now the two kids would sometimes meet me on the way to the woods: they didn't seem so shy of me any more.

"I wanted to see what sort of home they had, but they didn't seem to want to take me there; they said it was better to play where we always did. But one day I decided to go up to the house by myself, and they followed a little way behind. It was an ordinary sort of place, but there were no pastures or crops near by; the land was uncultivated and overgrown, and looked dreary and desolate. The door was open and when the children caught up with me we all went in together. The house was poorly lit and there was a musty smell about it. A woman came up to us, but didn't say anything by way of a greeting. Her eyes were hard and she kept them on me all the time, still not saying a word. There was something, I don't know exactly what, but there was something evil about her: she had tufts of hair hanging from her chin and her thick, bloodless lips were bitter and scornful. But none of this really worried me; I just thought well, so this is their mother, then I started looking round the room.

"'How did he get here?' she asked the children.

"'He plays with us in the woods,' they answered rather timidly.

"She looked at me curiously and, I thought, not quite so harshly as at first—or perhaps I was just getting used to her. For a moment I thought she looked like the girl when she first showed herself in the woods with those wide-open eyes.

"It took me a bit of time to get used to the dim light in there. I can't explain why exactly, but it was all very peculiar. The house wasn't all that different from ours—but still, it somehow wasn't the same. Every house has got its own smell about it, I know, but this one smelt raw and musty: it might have been because the rock face was so close, but there was this damp, cold smell about it. I walked around the room, thinking how strange it all was.

"There was a long sword hanging up in the corner, sort of hidden away. It was a double-edged sword, broad and straight it was, and there was a picture of the Virgin and Child on it, and all sorts of funny signs and letters. I'd never seen one like it before, so I went up to have a closer look, and I couldn't stop myself touching it. And then I heard a long groaning noise, and the sound of someone sobbing. I looked round and went over to the others.

"'Who's that crying?' I asked.

"'Crying? There's nobody crying,' said the mother. She stared at me and her eyes changed completely.

"'Come with me,' she said, and she took hold of my hand. She led me back to the corner and made me touch it like I'd done before. I heard the groaning and sobbing again, very clearly this time.

"'The sword!' she screamed, and she dragged me away from it. 'It's the sword!' She let go of me and turned to the stove and started stirring something in a pan.

"'Whose child are you?' she asked after a while, and she stroked her chin as she said it. I can remember thinking what a cruel mouth she had.

"'My father's Christopher from Våla,' I said.

"'Hmmm.'

"The kids' eyes were almost standing out of their heads with fright, and they just stood there rooted to the spot. She carried on with her food, but when she'd finished she drew up a stool, sat down and lifted me up on her lap. She stroked my hair a bit.

"'Yes,' she said, and she gave me a long, searching look. 'Yes, I'd better take you home.'

"She got herself ready and put on another skirt and a peculiar sort of hood I'd never seen a woman wear before. Then we set off.

"When we got to the woods she asked me 'Is this where you play?' and now and again she'd say a few words something like that as we walked along; and she held my hand when she saw I was scared. I didn't know what it was all about, and I didn't dare ask.

"As we were walking across the fields towards our house, mother came dashing out onto the doorstep. She was as white as a ghost: I'd never seen her so pale.

"'What are you doing with my child? Leave the boy alone, let him go I tell you, you filthy bitch!'

"As the woman snatched her hand away from mine her face twisted and she looked like a hunted beast.

"'What have you done to my boy?'

"'He's been up at our place. . . .'

"'You lured him into your . . . your defiled house!' my mother screamed.

"'No I did not: he came by himself, I'll have you know—and when he went to touch the sword we heard something sobbing and moaning.'

"Mother looked at me with a perplexed, terrified expression in her staring eyes.

"'I suppose you know what that means?' the woman asked.

"'No . . . no, I don't.'

"'It means that sooner or later that sword will be his death.'

"Mother let out a half-stifled scream and stared at me: she was as white as a sheet and her lips were trembling, but she didn't say a word.

"'Take your brat. I thought I'd be doing you a favour by warning you, but it seems I've just made you mad. You'll hear nothing more from us till his time comes, since that's the way you want it.'

"And she turned furiously and walked away.

"Mother took me in her trembling arms, pressed me to her and kissed me. But there was a stony, far-away look in her eyes. She took me indoors, then rushed out again, and I saw her running across the fields, shouting something.

"She came back with father, and they were both quiet and downcast. I can still remember how I stood at the window and watched them walk up by the roadside.

"Neither of them said a word to me. Mother started making something or other on the stove and father paced up and down the room without sitting down as he usually did. His thin face was rigid, tense, as if there was no life in it. When mother went out to draw some water he stood me in front of him and looked into my eyes in a furtive, searching way, and then turned away from me. They didn't talk to each other, either. After a while father went out, walked around the fields without doing anything in particular, and then just stood there looking out into the distance.

"A dismal, depressing time followed. I used to go out by myself in the daytime and no one seemed to bother about me. And nothing was like it had been before, not even the fields, although the sun was shining beautifully just as it had always done. I tried to play for a bit, but that wasn't any good either. When they were near me they'd walk by without saying anything: it was as if they didn't know me. But at night, when mother was putting me to bed, she'd hold me so tight against her I'd almost choke.

"I couldn't understand why everything was so different, so mournful. Even when I felt happy it still wasn't as it had been before. The whole farm was gloomy and silent, as if no one there ever said anything. But sometimes, when they thought I was too far away to listen, I could hear them whispering together. I'd no idea what I'd done, but I knew it was something awful, so awful they could hardly stand the sight of me. I tried to keep myself amused and stay away from them as much as I could, because I thought that was what they wanted.

"Mother's cheeks became hollow and she wouldn't eat anything; every morning her eyes were red from crying. I remember I spent a lot of time behind the barn and started building a house out of little stones, all by myself.

"One day, at last, mother called me to her, and father was there too. I went up to her and she took me by the hand and led me out into the woods, while father stayed behind and watched us go. I saw she was taking the same path I used to go by, and for the first time I was really frightened. But things were so miserable already that I thought they couldn't possibly get worse, so I just went along with her. I walked close up to her and tried to tread carefully among all the stones and roots, so that I wouldn't be a nuisance to her. Her face had become so thin you could hardly recognize her.

"When we got near the house she started trembling. I held her hand as tight as I could to try to cheer her up a bit.

"The woman and children were in the house, but this time there was a man there as well. He was well-built and rough-looking with big, thick lips with wrinkles on them, and his face was covered with pock-marks. His eyes were yellowish and heavy and bloodshot and he looked wild and cruel. I'd never seen anything that terrified me so much.

"No one said anything as we went in. The woman went to the stove and poked the coals so hard that the sparks flew up. The man glanced at us first and then turned away. Mother was standing in the doorway meekly asking them about something: it was something to do with me—I gathered that much—but I didn't know what. She kept saying there was 'a way', if only they'd take it.

"None of them answered her.

"She looked so miserable and wretched standing there that I thought they couldn't say no, whatever she was asking, but they didn't even look at her. It was just as if we weren't there.

"Mother talked the whole time, more and more pleadingly, in a low, desperate voice. She looked so pitiful, and tears came to her eyes as she told them I was her only child.

"And then she just stood there crying—but that didn't do any good either.

"I found the whole business so gruesome I didn't know what to do, so I went over to the children, who were huddled up in a corner. We exchanged frightened looks with each other, then sat down side by side on a bench by the wall; we were all so tired out we couldn't stand any longer.

"We sat for a long time in gloomy silence, then suddenly I jumped as the man spoke; he stood there looking at us all, but it was me he was talking to.

"'Come with me,' he said.

"I was shaking as I got off the seat, and when he went out I didn't dare do other than follow him, and mother came too, and the woman turned and jeered at her. But the man and I went alone down a well-trodden footpath leading to a small clump of birches beside the house. It felt queer walking with him, and I kept my distance all the time, but even so the ice seemed to break a bit. There was a spring in the clump: it must have been where they got their water from, because there was a scoop there. He knelt down beside it and filled his hand with the clear water. 'Drink,' he said.

"I could see he meant me no harm, so I did as he said and wasn't a bit afraid. You might think he looked even more frightening from close up, but in fact he looked kinder and more like ordinary people. He stayed on his knees and looked at me with those heavy, bloodshot eyes, and I remember thinking how he, too, looked anything but happy. He made me drink three times.

"'Now that you've drunk from my hand it's gone,' he said, 'and you needn't be afraid any longer.' And he ran his hand quickly through my hair.

"It was as if a miracle had happened.

"He got up and we went back again. The sun was shining, the birds were chirping in the birches with their sweet smell of leaves and bark, and there was mother waiting for us: her eyes shone with happiness when she saw us coming hand in hand. She clasped me to her and kissed me.

"'God bless you,' she said to the executioner, but he simply turned away.

"We went home happily."

When he had finished the others murmured to themselves thoughtfully.

"Yes, that's the way it is."

"Evil's a queer thing all right, there's no getting away from it."

"It's as if there was something, well, something good in it."

"That's true enough."

"And the power it's got! It can kill you or cure you, and that's the truth."

"That it can."

"It's a weird and wonderful thing all right."

"That was a fine story, a very fine story."

"But I still think your old lady should've made it up to the hangman's wife for calling her all those names."

"So do I: but she didn't."

"Didn't she, now?"

They sat for a while thinking about the story, took a pull at their tankards and wiped their mouths.

"Oh, the executioner's got his good side right enough. There's plenty of stories about how he's helped them as was in pain and sick, some of 'em so bad the doctors had given 'em up."

"And he knows what it is to suffer, too: he hurts himself when he does what he has to. And you know he always asks the victim to forgive him just before he does his business."

"Oh, he's got nothing against them he kills. They can be like old pals, I've seen 'em."

"Old pals, that's a laugh! I once saw 'em cuddling one another on the way up to the scaffold!"

"Get away!"

"Oh yes I did: they were both so pissed they could hardly walk. They'd drunk up all they could hold and more besides and it was as much as they could do to stagger up to the block. There wasn't much to choose between 'em, but I reckon of the two the hangman was the worse for wear. He let out a great 'Whee!' as he chopped the other bloke's head off!"

They had a good laugh and sat back drinking for a while.

"It's *your* head they should've had, if you ask me: well, it could happen to any of us one day, for that matter."

"Very true."

"But the things he can do! What you were just telling us about, it's like a miracle. If he hadn't freed you you'd have been a gonner by now."

"Oh he can work miracles all right: he's worse than any of your saints where that's concerned."

"Aah come on: it's the saints and the Virgin Mary as do all the real miracles."

"And Jesus Christ, who freed us from all our sins."

"I know that, you idiot, but what's that got to do with it? It's his lordship we're talking about."

"Yeah, there's power there: there's power in evil all right."

"But where do you think it all comes from? From the devil, if you ask me, and that's why people are so mad keen on it: they want it more than anything on earth, more than God's word or the sacrament even."

"But it helped our friend there."

"Yes, yes it did."

"As like as may be."

"And there's no priest as could've done it."

"Not on your life: it was up to the devil and his lot there, 'cause it was the devil as had got him."

"It's all the devil's work if you ask me."

"How do you mean?"

"Well, you heard him say yourself that the hangman turned away when his mother said 'God bless you'."

"Ugh!"

"Come on, for crying out loud, pack it in and let's have something to drink!"

"Good idea. Hey, let's have some more ale; more ale! And make it good and strong!"

"And take it out the proper barrel—oh no, not the one with the finger in: you *have* got a hanged man's finger in there, haven't you?"

The girl turned pale, shook her head and stammered out something.

"Come on, the whole town knows you have. Never mind, give it to us; we don't give a damn, so long as it's good and strong. 'Whee!' he said!"

"You watch yourself—one of these fine days you might not have a neck to pour more ale down!"

"In that case let's make hay while the sun shines!"

"The devil himself brewed this: you can tell by the taste."

"Oh, this is the devil's own den all right, but you won't find better ale anywhere."

They drank and spread themselves over the table, leaning on their elbows.

"Wonder if there's anything doing up at the scaffold tomorrow morning?" said the old shoemaker. "Is there anything in the wind?"

"I wonder."

"More than likely."

"It's just that his lordship's on his travels, all got up in his finery."

"I wouldn't be surprised."

"But there's no talk of anyone being done, is there?"

"Not as I've heard."

"You'll hear all right when they start banging the drum."

"Drink up and give it a rest, grandad."

They drank.

A young man came in, followed by a couple of women.

"Hallo, here come the tarts."

"Wherever his lordship goes it's birds of a feather."

"Hey, light up and let's have a look at the goods!"

"Nice-looking bits. Brothel girls?"

"What do you think?"

"Aren't you going to sit with his lordship over there? What's up—windy?"

"Or perhaps you know him too well?"

"Now then girls, if you go up to the scaffold you'll find a bloke hanging there without a stitch on him: they pinched his clothes last night and you can see everything the Good Lord blessed him with. You see enough as it is? There's women been coming all morning from miles around to see the show: nothing like a hanged man's bag of tricks, they say! What are you giggling at? You'd better watch yourselves with his lordship over there!"

"Hasn't he been down to have a whack at you yet?"

"He's been all right: they're in the pillory as much as they're out of it."

"One of these days he'll boot you out of town, and then you're going to have to get a move on if you want to keep your pretty backsides!"

One of the women turned on them.

"You shut your trap, Skinner, and go home to your old woman; she shares it around as much as us. Day before yesterday she was down our place offering herself out: said she couldn't get enough at home."

"And that's enough of your lip! If you think that's news to me, you're wrong: I know all about her goings on. But I'll flay her alive one of these days, you wait and see."

"A fat lot of good that'll do."

"I will, I'll do her in before she's much older!"

"That'll really please her: then she'll be able to get it from Old Nick himself!"

They had a good laugh at him as he sat there muttering.

"Women! they get away scot free, in this world and the next."

"Come on, they get their share of hell-fire and all the rest of it just like anyone else, if you ask me."

"Right enough: they don't cut any ice with his lordship there."

"Not likely."

"And you know there's many an executioner likes doing in women most of all."

"I don't wonder."

"Much better than a lot of stinking blokes, I bet!"

"You're telling me."

"I wouldn't say they *like* it—not always, anyway. I was watching an execution once and he just couldn't bring himself to get on with it."

"Go on!"

"Just couldn't do it, he couldn't: he fell for her head over heels right there at the block."

"He did *what*?"

"No!"

"Oh yes he did. Everyone there could see it. He just stood there looking at her and couldn't even lift the axe."

"She was a fine-looking girl, too: I can still remember her long black hair and those soft, dangerous eyes, scared and watery like an animal's; and her face—it was so uncommon lovely, I can see it to this day. No one really knew her, because she was a stranger and she'd only just come to town; and he'd never set eyes on her before, but it wasn't surprising she had such an effect on him: his face was all white and his hand shook. 'I can't,' he said, and it was so loud the people nearest the gallows heard it clearly."

"No!"

"It was a fantastic sight, it really was. And when they saw the love in his eyes they were touched and started whispering and talking to one another about it, and everyone seemed to think what a terrible pity it all was."

"You can understand why."

"That you can. Well, he stood there for a while, then he put his axe down and went up to her and took her hand. The tears came to her eyes: it was as if she'd fallen in love too; and no wonder when you think what he was doing for her, him as was to kill her and all."

"Mm."

"But what happened in the end?"

"Well, he went up to the judge and told him and everyone else there that he'd marry her: and you know that when anything like that happens they can grant pardons if they've a mind to, and people started saying as how they thought she should be let off. And everyone there, the judge included, seemed to be uplifted when they saw the wonderful things love can do, even at the gallows, and lots of them were moved to tears. And so that was that: the priest gave them his blessing and they were man and wife.

"But she had to be branded with the sign of the gallows, for that's the law, and the gallows has to have its victim one way or another. But it saved her, as I say."

"It's almost unbelievable."

"You can say that again."

"What happened to them afterwards—I mean could they really be happy after all that?"

"Oh yes. They lived together in his house and were the happiest couple you could ever hope to find, everyone said so. They said they'd never had a hangman like it.

His love for her had changed him so much, and life was completely different in the house from what it had been before: well, you know what sort of people usually live in places like that. I often used to see them together when she was expecting her child: they were just like any other couple in love and she was a fine-looking woman, in spite of having to wear a hood, like all executioners' wives; and she had that ugly mark on her forehead of course, but like I say, she was still lovely to look at."

"When the baby was due they tried to get hold of a midwife, like everyone does; it seems they were looking forward to the child just like ordinary people: that's what people said, anyway. But they couldn't find one, I remember it happening, because they asked the woman who lived opposite us; they were very keen to have her in case anything went wrong, but she wouldn't go, and nor would anyone else, because it meant going to a tainted house."

"It's still not a Christian thing to do, refusing to help like that."

"But don't you see, it would mean unclean work, and then she might have to go and see to a decent woman after."

"Yes, that's true."

"Well, so she had to stay all by herself; it all happened so suddenly that he didn't manage to get to her in time, and that didn't make things any easier. No one knows exactly the ins and outs of what happened, but she admitted later to the judge that she'd strangled the child."

"Get away! But *did* she?"

"But why should she?"

"She's supposed to have said that when she'd got enough strength back after the birth to see to the baby a bit she wiped the blood off its face and saw a birthmark on its forehead—a gallows. You see, when they branded her it hurt an awful lot, and she was still in pain when she got pregnant, she said. Then she said she didn't want the child to live in this world, that he was branded already, and she loved him so much and so on and so forth, and there was no sense in what she was saying, so I heard; it's plain the poor thing was fated to do evil."

"What an awful thing to happen."

"It certainly was."

"She was condemned to be buried alive, for this was no small matter she had on her conscience now, and her husband had to fill in her grave. I was there and watched it: of course it was hard for him, he'd loved her all the time, that's for sure, and he couldn't do his duty right even now, even after the terrible thing she'd done. He stood looking at her beautiful body as it disappeared under the shovelfuls of earth, and he didn't cover her face until he had to. She didn't utter a single word the whole time—I suppose they must have said goodbye to each other before—but just lay there gazing at him lovingly. When at last he was forced to throw earth over her face he looked away. It was a terrible thing for him to have to do, but he had to do it: that was what the law decreed.

"Some say he went out late that night and tried to dig her up again, in case she was still alive, but that's a lot of rubbish: he must have known she was dead.

"Soon afterwards he left the district and no one knew what became of him."

"But what an awful thing to happen."

"Yes, but they should have known that that's the way it is with folk like themselves—I mean, the baby *had* to be marked, just like they had to themselves."

"There was nothing peculiar about the kid having the gallows-mark."

"No, it's on 'em from the very start."

"Course it is."

"And there's nothing anyone can do about *that*."

"So he had to kill her after all."

"Yes."

"Well, that's the way it was to be from the start."

There was a great din outside the door and a man staggered in, shouting at someone out in the darkness and furiously shaking what was left of an arm.

"That's a pack of lies: you counted 'em yourself, you village idiot, you saw it was all right."

"Them dice was loaded, you thieving swine."

"Like hell they were! Were they loaded, Jack?"

"Not on your life!" answered a young boy who was following close on the handless man's heels.

"That little devil's in on it too, you filthy cripple: it's him as holds your cards and does all the other things you can't do yourself. And them cards was marked too, or you'd never have got my money."

"Aw, drop dead, you yokel!"

He sat down at a table and glanced around. When he saw the executioner his face twitched: it was a thin face, with sunken cheeks and wide, staring eyes. The boy edged up to him on the seat.

"So the old gallows-bird's on his travels again, then."

"What's up, Lasse? You scared of sitting by his lordship, too?"

"Like hell I am!"

He went slowly up to the table and sat down at the far end. The boy crept after him.

"And that's just where you belong, you filth!" shouted the farmer. "He'll have you good and proper before you're much older!"

"He's right, Lasse, it's your head next time: there's nothing else left to cut off!"

"You're talking shit, and that's about your limit, too. They'll never have *my* head off!"

"Oh no?"

"You want to bet?"

He sat up at the table and shrugged his shoulders.

"Give me some ale!" he shouted to the girl, and she hurried up to him with a jug. The boy held it up to his mouth and he took a long pull at it. The boy waited for him to get his breath, and then gave him more.

"So I cheated you, did I?" he said, turning slowly to the farmer, who had sat down by the door.

"Yes, you did."

"Do you really think I have to cheat to get my hands on your measly pennies? They come running straight into my pockets 'cause they can't stand the stink of your filthy old pants!"

"Shut your face!"

They all laughed at the farmer, who was now at a loss for words.

"Old Lasse there doesn't have to load his dice or mark his cards if he hasn't a mind to."

"No, he's got a lot of other tricks up his sleeve, and old yokels like you can't beat him at *them*!"

"He's as good at the game as anyone else in the business, is old Lasse; but I don't know how he manages it all, the way he is."

"Oh don't you worry about old Lasse: he gets by all right."

"You can say that again."

"I remember the time they cut my fingers off, when I was about his age," he said, pointing to the boy. "I was there when they was nailed up on the pillory, and I had a good laugh. 'Well,' they said, 'you won't be cheating nobody with *them* no more.' But I just laughed and told 'em I couldn't care less. Lasse'll be all right, says I, and that's just how it's been."

He blinked heavily two or three times, and his face twitched. He wanted more ale, so he nudged the boy with the stump of his arm, and the boy hurriedly lifted the tankard. He had a wide-awake little face and his eyes darted to and fro: he noticed everything that went on.

"But what about when they cut your hands off? That was another kettle of fish."

"D'you think that worried me? Not on your life!"

He wiped his mouth on his sleeve. The old shoemaker at the other end of the table leaned forward. His voice was hoarse with excitement.

"You know he's got the mandrake?" he whispered.

"No, it's just the same for me," Lasse continued, loud and clear. "I don't worry about it; and I've got the lad here, and he's got the knack all right!"

"I bet he has, too."

The boy blinked, pleased with the praise.

"Is he your own, Lasse?"

"Search me, I don't know. But it's more than likely—he takes after me all right."

"You don't know?"

"Not really. His real mother's Hanna the whore, but he ran away from her 'cause she used to give him a good hiding instead of a good feed, and now he sticks to me as can teach him a bit about how to look after himself in life. And he's so easy to teach, you've never seen anything like it. Am I your dad, Jacky boy?"

"It don't matter to me either way," the boy grinned.

"That's my boy! Who gives a damn? But you're all right with me, aren't you?"

"You bet!" The boy grinned again.

"Come on, Lasse, you won't kid me you can manage with just that snotty-nosed little brat."

"Why not?"

"No, come on!"

"I reckon you must have more powerful friends than him."

"And who might they be?"

"How should I know?"

"Yeah, how should you know. What sort of shit are you talking now?"

For a while nobody said a word. They just sat there fidgeting, fingering their tankards.

"Is it true you've got the mandrake root?"

"Oh, give it a rest!"

"No, I suppose you couldn't have dug it up, the state you're in."

Lasse's staring eyes pierced the half-darkness and his thin face looked even more drawn.

"Lasse can manage worse things than that when he has to."

"You bet he can."

"But fancy him digging it up under the scaffold—no hands and all!"

"Yes; and when you hear that scream, when you hear that—then you know you're done for."

They looked at him: his head was jerking violently and he could not stop twitching.

"He's got the mandrake root and a lot more besides, has old Lasse there. I reckon you sold yourself to Old Nick a long time back, Lasse."

"That's right—I did!"

"What did I tell you!"

"Just listen to that, then!"

"But don't the evil spirits come and haunt you at night?"

"Get away! Not when you're hand-in-glove with Old Nick, they don't. You can sleep like a new-born babe."

"Come off it, Lasse, that's the limit!"

"Yeah, that's laying it on *too* thick: and if you and him's such good pals, what do you go around in that state for?"

"His lordship's seen to you like you belonged to *him*, not Old Nick!"

They laughed at their own jokes, and the cripple glared at them with burning, hateful eyes.

"What do I care?"

"You mean you don't?"

"Looks to me like they've carved you up like ordinary gallows-meat, Old Nick or no Old Nick!"

"So what? But they won't finish Lasse off, you can be sure of that!" His voice had risen to a screech and his eyes were bulging. "Oh no, they won't find that so easy, believe you me!"

"Won't they? Well, it looks like they've got off to a pretty good start!"

"They've taken nothing from me—nothing!" he screamed, getting to his feet. "Because they can't, do you hear, they can't! There's no power on earth can touch me, no power on earth!"

"What the hell are you on about now? That's just about the end!"

"They'll never get me. What I've got is stronger than the lot of'em, and when I've gone, the lad here'll inherit it."

"What's that, Lasse? Got things to leave, have you? Just listen to that!"

"That's right, I have: and a damn site more than any of you have. When I go he'll get the mandrake and he'll get the whole of hell too!"

"So you *have* got the mandrake!"

"Yes, damn you, yes I have. Do you want to see it?"

"No, for God's sake!"

"I wear it round my neck here; shaped just like a man it is, and the bloke what's got it can have anything he wants: he can steal and he can get away with anything, hands or no hands!"

They were all staring at him, their mouths agape and fear in their eyes.

"But how did a bloke like you get hold of it? You didn't go . . . up by the scaffold!"

"Where else? Right under the scaffold itself, where they bury the bodies when they fall down."

"You mean you went *there*? At *night*?"

"Course I did! And there's none of you with the guts to

go through with it, either: it wasn't like cuddling up to mummy and saying your prayers—not likely!"

"No fear!"

"The way they moaned and groaned enough to scare the . . ."

"Who?"

"The dead, you fool: who else? You should have seen the way they went for me and tried to get hold of me as I was looking for it! I beat 'em off as best I could, and then they howled and screamed like a crowd of halfwits being flogged in the madhouse. They was moaning and screeching like the very devils of hell, and I just couldn't get rid of 'em; they went on and on, till I thought I was going mad myself. 'Get away, damn you, get away!' I shouted; 'I'm not one of you, I'm alive! I need it!' And in the end I managed to fight 'em off. Then I saw it. It was growing there right under the scaffold, where Petter the butcher and a few others was still strung up. I shifted some of the earth with one of my stumps; then I laid down on the ground and got it between my teeth."

"You didn't!"

"Oh yes I did. What do you think the others do, them as what's too scared to go 'emselves? They send their dogs, right?"

His eyes were ablaze and wild.

"But then it screamed: it screamed and it screamed, enough to freeze your very blood! But I hadn't plugged up my ears, not me; I wasn't like the usual half-hearted cowards, oh no, I let it scream and I pulled it up and up till I got to the root. And then came the smell, the smell of blood and decay, and all the howling and bellowing of hell. But I didn't cover my ears, I pulled and I pulled: *because I wanted it and I was going to have it*!"

He was raving like one possessed, and they backed away from him.

"And when I'd got it the whole sky thundered and the

earth shook around me; the abyss opened and the bodies and blood of the dead came floating up; the darkness was split open and fire poured out over the whole earth! The noise, the horrible noise, it was as if all hell had been let loose on earth: and everything, everything was on fire! 'I've got it!' I shouted. '*Now* I've got it!'"

He stood shaking the stumps of his arms above his head like some frightful, deformed evil spirit; there was an uncontrollable madness in his eyes and his voice was no longer that of a human being.

"I've got my legacy to leave, damn you, I've got my legacy!"

The executioner sat motionless, his heavy, timeless eyes gazing out into the darkness before him.

There were a lot of people in the night-club, milling around in the half-light among the sounds of voices, laughter and the clinking of glasses; in the middle of the room couples were dancing slowly to soft music under the dim greenish and violet light cast by the slowly revolving globe in the ceiling.

More people got up to dance in between the tables and soon the whole room was filled with women in brightly coloured dresses holding on to men with their eyes half closed, all dancing to the rhythm of the jazz-band.

A pretty woman with an attractive figure turned and looked over her partner's shoulder.

"I say, just look—the executioner's here," she said. "How fascinating!"

The light swept over the guests, casting a pale, septic green colour on the tables, perspiring waiters rushed to and fro among the chatter and laughter, champagne corks popped.

A fat man with a crumpled shirtfront came forward and bowed politely.

"It's a great honour for us, having the executioner here,"

he said, obsequiously rubbing his hands and adjusting the pince-nez in front of his little beady eyes.

The dance ended and the couples went back smiling to their tables.

"Do you know who's here? The executioner!"

"No, really?"

"Yes, there he is, over there."

"Well, that's really something!"

A young man with an intense expression on his child-like face stepped up in front of the executioner, came to attention and raised his arm in salute. "Heil!" he shouted, and stood there rigidly for a while before turning, clicking his heels and going back to his seat.

While the talking and laughter went on, a scruffy man came in and went from table to table holding out his bony hand and mumbling something, until he was shown to the door. Seedy-looking young men sat sipping their drinks.

"Don't you think he looks smart in those red clothes?"

"He certainly does."

"And so cruel."

"Looks a proper pimp, if you ask me."

"Don't talk such rot; he's a wonderful man."

"Why does he sit there with his hand on his forehead all the time?"

"How should I know?"

"He's marvellous, just marvellous."

"He certainly is."

"What do you think it's like, being an executioner?"

"Fabulous, I bet."

The music struck up again, a slow, languishing tune played by a new band. The couples moved out into the meandering blue light, the women draping their slender arms over their partners' shoulders, pairs of narrowed eyes looking half asleep.

"Anything special on tomorrow?"

"Not as far as I know, but I've heard they've rounded

up quite a few they're thinking of bumping off: good luck to them, I say."

"Nothing wrong in that. There's plenty more around—good, decent ones, too. It's always the best who survive, that's plain enough."

"Couldn't agree more."

An elderly, military-looking man strutted confidently up to the executioner's table, smacking his lips.

"Excellent, sir, the way they're putting things right. People must damn well learn to behave themselves!"

"What the hell's this! We ordered dry and they have the cheek to bring us demi-sec: whatever next!"

"I'm terribly sorry. . . ."

"That's all very well, but what service! And after having to wait for it for hours."

"*And* he's opened it."

"Just you go and change it; we never drink anything but dry."

A well-fed businessman's wife waddled out of the ladies' room and clapped her hands together when she caught sight of the executioner.

"Well, just fancy that—the executioner's here! Just *wait* till I tell Herbert!"

She went up to him and put her hand affably on his arm.

"My son's just dying to meet you: he's so fond of bloodshed, dear boy."

She got up and looked around in a motherly way for her family.

The music continued playing dreamily, caressing the slender bodies of the dancing women. A small, dirty boy slipped in among the chattering guests and went around the tables opening his ragged coat to show he had nothing on underneath, until the waiters got hold of him and threw him out.

"On the contrary, sir, violence is the highest expression of man's physical—and spiritual—powers. Thanks to us, everyone's beginning to realize this at last. And if anyone thinks otherwise we'll convince him all right, by using just those powers. He'll believe us then, don't you think?"

"You bet he will."

"We hope so."

"As I was saying: we shall insist on castration for anyone who won't see things our way. It's essential if our ideas are to prevail—it's as simple as that. Surely you can't want us to let such filth contaminate the generations of the future? Oh no, my good sir, we know where our responsibilities lie."

"Of course we do."

"But my dear fellow, you're so ridiculously behind the times with these old-fashioned ideas. You must realize that there will simply never be any other way of looking at things again but our way: and that, you see, is that!"

"I suppose if you put it that way . . . I suppose I do see it more clearly. Yes . . . yes, of course I do."

"Now look: if you can just stop thinking as people have always thought in the past, you'll begin to understand this completely new way we have of looking at things. It's a little difficult at first, I know, but basically it's all really so simple."

"I suppose it must be."

"Have you ever seen one of the opposition get a really good thrashing, like we do it in our part of the country? I promise you, it's the most uplifting sight you could ever hope to see: you feel as if you're playing a part in raising civilization to a higher form of life, making it noble."

"I'd certainly like to see it."

"Do you know, we've managed to convert old fellows of up to eighty if we've kept it up long enough."

"Incredible! And when you think how difficult it usually is to get people to accept anything."

"Oh yes. What we're achieving is something quite unique, that I assure you.

"And we're fully aware of our responsibility to future generations *for all time*, you understand. We know the time is ripe now: if people start thinking in the right way now, they'll never be misled again. We mustn't forget that we're living in a time of greatness, a crucial period for all mankind, a time on which the continuation of life on earth depends."

"Yes, yes indeed."

"And *we* are responsible for that, you understand.

"They talk about class—there's no such thing any more. And that's what's so great, so magnificent in what I've been telling you about. There are only people who think like us—and a few sitting around in certain places being taught to think as we do; and those who come out again have certainly learned!

"You can see for yourself: people are sitting here drinking champagne—or perhaps just a glass of beer, most of them—workers, middle-class people, and some better off than either; they're all here together and there's no difference between them. And they all think in exactly the same way—*our* way. Everyone you see here thinks just like us!"

"I suppose they must."

"You have before you, in fact, the magnificent, unique sight of one assembled, united people: even the misguided few will be integrated soon, there's no question of it. We'll sort out the awkward ones all right! Ours is a people united, standing outside its prisons confidently waiting for the cries of the converted."

"But what a spirit: this is something really thrilling!"

"The world has never seen anything like it. It's like mass worship, with crowds of people devoutly waiting to hear the shrieks of the misguided as he's reformed; they feel such deep veneration for what's happening to their race there, behind closed doors. It's really a very moving sight, and it's only here, in our country, that this could possibly happen. There's no other people on earth to match us, not one bit.

"And we must create our own god, and do so without delay. Our people can't be expected to worship a god who's been the idol of other, inferior races. We are a deeply religious people, but we need a god of our own. The idea of one deity for everyone is a blatant mockery of our whole philosophy, and will be punished in future just like any other crime."

In the semi-darkness a nasty-looking individual with an insolent grin on his face could be seen going from table to table, begging; when people refused to give him anything he knocked against their table, upsetting the drinks.

A group of people were sitting at a table in one of the far corners of the room.

"What the hell's this! We order beer and sausages and you bring us champagne: whatever next! What do you think we are, bloody millionaires like those bastards there?"

"I beg your pardon, gentlemen, I thought you were upper-class people. . . ."

"Like hell we are! Open your eyes next time, or I'll give you something that'll wake you up!"

A soldier slouched into the room, sat down at the executioner's table and immediately began trying to rile him.

"What are you all got up in that stupid rigout for? Why aren't you in uniform, eh? Just look at him!"

"Shhh!" whispered someone sitting near by. "Can't you see who he is?"

"Course I can see; but he looks bloody stupid, if you ask me. So that's the executioner, is it? So what, what can *he* do? It's machine-guns and grenades that do the work, not the likes of him. You've got no idea, mate, I can tell by just looking at you."

"Don't talk such rot. He knows his job all right—a damn sight better than you know yours. You'd better lay off, lad: he and you are in the same business, let me tell you."

"All right, but why doesn't he use a machine-gun? That's what he wants, a good modern weapon: he could really get going with that! You should be in uniform, old chap!"

"Oh, give it a rest, boy. The way you talk, anyone can tell you've seen less action than my old pisspot!"

"But I'll see some action all right, you can be bloody sure of that. And then you'll see the devil in me!"

"Oh yes, when *you* get going the sparks'll *really* fly!"

"Me and the other boys, I mean. We know a thing or two about fighting, believe you me, and we're not scared of getting down to it, either!"

"Well said, lad!"

"The boy's all right; he's just had a drop too much beer for his age. It's a great thing the country's got young people like him; it does an old man's heart a power of good to see it."

"Oh, the way you old men go on: you're all out of touch. Cheers, hangman, you're my type! There's you and me to sort out the world, anyway. Well, drink then, you miserable devil, what's up with you?"

A party at one of the tables burst out laughing, and the other guests and the waiters turned to see what was going on. One of the young women was completely doubled up.

"We've got to have a war, we've got to. War means health, and any country that doesn't want it is a sick country!"

"That's right: peace is all very well for little kids and for the sick—they need it. But it's not for full-grown, healthy men and women.

"There's only one place for a self-respecting man, and that's the trenches. We ought to live in trenches even in peacetime: living in houses makes people soft.

"We need a war, a bloodbath! No healthy people can

do without one for more than ten years at the very longest; otherwise they begin to degenerate, if they're a healthy people, that is."

"Yes, and those who bring wars to an end are traitors."

"Right!"

"Down with traitors! Down with traitors!"

"Hang them!"

"Yes, hang them, even if they've won the war. If they end it they throw the whole nation into all the uncertainty of peace, with no consideration for anyone. We all know what war means, but a nation at peace is threatened by all the unknown dangers imaginable."

"He's right!"

"Let's free ourselves from the corruption of all this mollycoddling. We must bring our children up to be soldiers: when they learn to walk they must learn to march like soldiers, not toddle behind their mothers."

"That's easily done: *we'll* look after the nation's babies, instead of leaving them to the mercies of irresponsible parents."

"Let's do that!"

"Then we can regard the future as assured."

"Yes!"

A man got up unsteadily from his seat: his face had been damaged so badly by shrapnel that only the lower half was recognizable; the rest was just a mass of red scars.

"Comrades-in-arms," he said, "I hear you talking about war, and it makes me so happy! I only hope I shall be allowed to live to see the proud day when our nation sets out again for the old battlefields. And I hope by then modern science will have advanced so far that even I can be among you. Someone's been reading me a book that's just come out, and it says there that it might not be long before we can see with our spirits; and actually fight with them! When that happens you'll find me right up in the front line, with an aim as good as the best of you: because my spirit, comrades-in-arms, my spirit is as whole as it ever was!"

"Bravo! Bravo!"

"Spoken like a man!"

"Magnificent!"

"It's only in times of greatness you find people like him."

"They say war gives a man's face the stamp of honour: there's the living proof of it."

"Wonderful!"

"What a nation! We're invincible!"

"And we must spread our message all over the world; it would be a terrible thing just to keep it to ourselves. And if any country refuses to accept it, we shall simply exterminate them."

"Of course we shall: for their own sakes. People who try to live without what we have to teach them are better off dead."

"Naturally."

"The world will thank us when it realizes what we mean."

"It's absolutely essential that people should keep up with the times and destroy what they have created in the past: it's what every healthy child does, after all. And destruction is far more important than the simple, routine business of construction. We are living in an age of greatness, an age of which to be proud! There will always be plenty of busy little sloggers building and building, there's no need to worry on that score. But the courageous ones, the men of spirit who wipe out everything in mankind's fairy-tale world at one swoop, so that we can begin again from scratch, these men come once in a million years—when we deserve them!

"Our people are healthy through and through, and that's why we have the moral courage to say quite openly that we love what others call oppression. It's only races of degenerate weaklings that want to be free from it. All powerful nations like to have someone standing over them with the whip: they thrive on it!"

"Absolutely right! And the most inspiring sight of all is that of the young people in our ranks. These fearless, hard-hearted young men and women of today are the very basis of our society: everywhere you can see them joining us, joining ranks with the powerful! Our young heroes. . . ."

"How *very* brave of them!"

"What was that? No? I thought I heard something."

Then people started whispering to each other and began getting up, raising their arms in salute; everyone's eyes were fixed on the door, where there were signs of great activity. The whole club was filled with a roar of acclamation:

"Long live the killers!"

Two well-dressed young men, quite ordinary, nice-looking individuals, walked in between the rows of outstretched hands, acknowledging their welcome by bowing politely and smiling left and right. Every single person in the club was on his or her feet, and they remained standing as the dance-music stopped and the more dignified orchestra played an anthem. Three waiters hurried silently up to the new arrivals and the head waiter, who was close behind them, upset some beer-mugs and a decanter of red wine over some ladies, who quickly and quietly dismissed his hurried apologies as he continued on his way. There was nowhere to sit, but a group of people was soon told to go home, and the young men settled down at their table.

"Every bloody place is the same: as soon as we turn up we're recognized."

"Yes, blast it," said his companion, blowing out cigarette smoke as he stretched his legs under the table and waited for their order to come. "It's beginning to be a bit of a drag, if you ask me."

"Yes, if we'd known what a nuisance it would be, being a killer, I don't reckon we'd ever have shot that bloke. They say he was a good sort, too."

"Yes, but you could tell just by looking at him that he wasn't one of us."

"Yes, he was a swine of a specimen."

The negroes had struck up their jazz again, and a thin woman carrying a baby wrapped in a shawl was walking around the room. Nobody noticed her, not even the staff, and after a while she left.

"You coming to help shift the bodies tonight?"

"Bodies?"

"A few traitors who didn't see eye-to-eye with us over the new order. We're shifting their bodies from the churchyard to a swamp: much more suitable place."

"Oh, I. . . ."

"What do you mean? Don't you want to help?"

"Well, I don't know; what's the idea?"

"Idea? Our movement's idea, my friend!"

"Yes, but . . . well, they were dead before we got into this."

"So what?"

"Well, it's a bit much to ask."

"What did you say? So you *won't* help: you refuse!"

"I didn't say that: I just said I thought it was a bit much."

"A bit much? Maybe you think it's a stupid idea?"

"No, I didn't mean that exactly."

"Well, what *did* you mean? Come on, out with it!"

"Well, I meant . . . bloody hell, lay off!"

"You're refusing to obey orders! I suppose you've got your own petty little ideas, have you?"

"Let me go, will you!"

"Oh no, that's not so easily done here."

"Let go of me, you swine!"

"Did you hear what he called us!"

"You cheeky little bastard! So you dare disobey, do you? Perhaps you're thinking of going over to the others?"

"I didn't disobey!"

"Yes you did!"

"Come on, there's no point arguing with a traitor. Let's settle the matter here and now."

A shot rang out, followed by a dull thud.

"Get rid of the body."

"Oh leave it: it's not in anyone's way."

The jazz played on, and a young woman with a slender neck turned round.

"Is something wrong?" she asked.

"Someone got shot, that's all."

"I see."

A group of people was sitting at a table hidden away in the shadows.

"You know what I reckon's going to happen tomorrow —what all the talk's about?"

"What?"

"Something those louts over there aren't expecting."

"What, then?"

"Well. . . ."

He rolled a cigarette and lit it from another one, spitting out little bits of tobacco.

"We can use a gun too, when we have to; God knows, we're the ones that taught them their tricks—as if they needed teaching!"

"Oh, it comes natural these days."

"You can say that again."

"It would be great to weed out a few more, don't you think? There's plenty who need it."

"You can count me in there."

A young woman came quietly in and sat down at the executioner's table. She looked like a beggar-woman, but when she took the shawl off her head a strange, deep light radiated from her face. She put her hand gently on his arm and he turned and looked at her—the only person he had looked at the whole time. We shall hear more of her later.

The music changed as the orchestra at the other end of the club struck up a slow tango based on an old classical tune. Everything was calm and the atmosphere nostalgic, but then a man had to go out to the toilet. When he came back he caught sight of the negro musicians sitting at a table behind their dais, hurriedly snatching a bite to eat. His face turned purple as he went up to them.

"What the hell do you mean by this, you swine: sitting here eating among white people!"

They turned around in surprise. The one closest to him began to get up. "What do you mean, sir?"

"What do I mean? And you have the effrontery to sit here eating, you filthy animal!"

The negro was on his feet in a flash, his eyes blazing, but he dared not do anything.

"Look at this, gentlemen, just look at this!" the white man screamed furiously across the room. People came hurrying forward and clustered around him and the negroes. "Have you ever seen anything like it? It's beyond all belief: these animals are sitting here eating amongst us —*us*!"

There was a tremendous uproar.

"What infernal impudence! I've never heard anything like it. Are we in the monkey-house or what? Just look at them!"

"We've got to eat just like anyone else," said one of the negroes.

"But not in the same place as people, you swine."

"Eat! You're not here to eat, you're here to play."

"You're privileged to play for us since we choose to be entertained by your music. And now watch your manners, or you might get strung up—is that clear?"

"Now get back to your places."

"Come on—what are you waiting for?"

The negroes showed no sign of doing as they were told.

"This, gentlemen, is passive resistance at its very worst," said a dignified, distinguished-looking man.

"Well, are you going to get on with it or aren't you?"

"Go on, get up on the stage!"

"We're hungry: if we're going to play we've got to eat."

"Hungry! Have you ever heard anything like it?"

"Yes, we've got to eat and we're entitled to," said a big, powerful negro with a threatening glare.

"Entitled! So you're entitled to things, are you?"

"Yes I am," said the negro, advancing on him.

"You dare to answer a white man like that, you impudent pup!" And the white man hit him full in the face.

The negro cringed, quivering like a wild beast. Then he leapt forward as quick as lightning and punched the white man so hard that he fell flat on his back.

What followed was pandemonium. Everyone in the place came rushing up to the stage and the club seethed in the wildest imaginable frenzy. The negroes shrank back together in a huddle, crouching and terrified, their eyes bloodshot and their white teeth bared, like some fantastic animals in a human jungle. A shot rang out and one of them tore into the white mob, screaming and lashing out in all directions like a madman, his blood pouring from him. Then came the others in a yelling mass, but they were stopped as the revolvers blazed away in unison and their wounds forced them to take cover behind tables and chairs.

"Now play, damn you, play!" screamed a good-looking man with fair hair, firing his Browning in the direction of their hiding-place as he spoke.

"No!" shouted the negroes.

"Look, we've got another band," someone called out

in an attempt to calm them down. "We can still have music."

"To hell with that sentimental slush! These bastards are going to play. Now get up, you apes!"

They were forced into the open and the furore began again, only more violently than before. Everything was thrown into an insane frenzy, with all manner of objects hurtling through the air like deadly missiles and the mob standing shrieking on their chairs. The negroes were hounded from one end of the room to the other.

"Stop, for God's sake stop: we're civilized just like you."

"What! Say that word once more and I'll damn well shoot you down."

"Civilized my foot!"

A big strapping negro, most probably the one who had struck the first blow, went through the place like one possessed, kicking over everything in his path and dealing out deadly punches left and right, till he was felled by a well-aimed shot; he clutched at his chest and slumped to the floor with a broad, vacant grin on his face. The others gathered what was left of their strength, picked up chairs and cracked the skulls of anyone and everyone within reach. They fought in blind fury, hatred blazing out of the whites of their eyes, till they dropped. "Biting are you, you little coward?" roared one of the uniformed fighters at a negro who lay half dead on the floor with his teeth round the white man's leg; then he lowered his revolver and put a bullet through him. The negroes shouted eerie, terrifying war cries like noises from the jungle, but they did not deter the whites, who held their own with their weapons, and the pistol-shots followed each other like machine-gun fire. It was like a full-scale battle.

The two young murderers took no part in it all, but sat looking on at their entertainment: they had done their bit.

At last those of the negroes who were still alive were pinned down in a corner and blocked in. They could hold out no longer, and there was nothing left but unconditional surrender.

"Got them!" the whites panted.

"Get up there!"

The negroes were driven up onto the stage and forced to take up their instruments.

A powerfully-built man in a dinner-jacket sat astride a chair facing them and pointed his revolver.

"Anyone who won't play gets this," he said.

And the negroes played: they played like madmen, their eyes ablaze and their hands and faces covered with blood; their music was frenzied, savage and horrifying, as blood-curdling as the sounds of nocturnal beasts and the thundering of the drums of death when the tribes of the jungle gather together after nightfall; such music had never been heard before. A massive negro stood at the fore with his teeth clenched, beating a crescendo on his drums as if in the grasp of all the devils in hell; there was a gaping wound running from the crown of his head to his neck, and his shirt was stained bright red. His bloody fists beat and beat again in tune with the instruments, creating a single discordant uproar.

"Fantastic, fantastic!" The whites danced, leapt and jumped about to the music, they danced in every corner of the place: it was like a witches' sabbath at its climax. Their faces were flushed with the aftermath of the battle and the heat of the room, the pungent smell of sweat drifted about mustily, the last gasps of dying men could be heard between the tables and the victims were trodden underfoot by the wildly dancing couples. The light in the ceiling whirled round, sweeping its multicoloured glow over the seething mass. The women shone with beauty and desire, devouring the big bleeding negro with hungry eyes and thrusting their legs between those of their partners; the men pressed their stomachs hard against the women, excited by their looks and by the hot revolvers which swung between their thighs like a second smouldering member. They had worked themselves up into an insane frenzy.

A man jumped up onto a table near where the executioner was sitting: his collar had been ripped off in the fight and his face was flushed in wild ecstasy as he waved his revolver above his head.

"Victory, comrades, victory! This is what happens to those who think they can get the better of us. Order and discipline are the victors' weapons, and on these we are building our empire."

He continued shouting and waving his arms, and a crowd gathered round to listen to him.

"And on this proud day, a day on which we have proved the superiority of our race to any other, we have the honour and pleasure to have among us the representative of that which we prize most highly in life: the executioner is here in our midst! We are honoured to have him here, for his presence shows—in case we needed showing—that our time is one of greatness; it's a sign that the old days of shame and unmanly weakness are a thing of the past, that a new day is about to dawn for mankind. His magnificent presence fills us with confidence and courage: he will lead us and we will follow him—him and him alone!

"We salute you, our leader, with these sacred emblems, these symbols of what is for us most holy and precious in life and which will introduce a new era in the history of mankind. Mankind's colour is the colour of blood! And we know we are worthy of you; we know you can be sure of us as we salute you: long live the executioner!"

He leapt down from the table, flushed and breathless, and walked up to the man to whom he was paying homage.

The executioner looked at him without raising his head. He made no move, gave no answer.

This seemed to disconcert the ardent admirer somewhat, and he was not quite sure what to say next. "Long live the executioner!" he shouted again, a little hesitantly this time, with his arm raised in salute. The others followed his example.

The executioner looked at them in silence.

"But . . . but aren't you the executioner?" they asked uncertainly.

The man they were addressing took his hand away from his forehead where the executioner's mark was branded: an ecstatic murmur went through the crowd.

"Yes, I am the executioner." He came to his feet and towered over them, a terrifying sight in his blood-red uniform. Everyone's eyes were on him, the shouting and screaming stopped and the room became so quiet that they could hear the sound of his breathing.

"I started my work when time itself began; I have been at it ever since that day, and it is likely to be as long again before I am finished. The centuries pass by, nations arise and vanish again into the night; but I do not grow old, and I alone remain and watch them go, with their blood on my hands. I follow mankind faithfully, and there is nowhere man has trodden, however remote, where I have not laid waste the land and stained the earth with blood. I have been with you since your creation and I shall be with you until your time on earth runs out. When you first looked up to the heavens and sought a god, I sacrificed one of your brothers. I still remember the wind howling through the trees, and the light from the fire flickering across your faces as I tore out his heart and gave it to the flames. Since then I have sacrificed men and women without number, guilty and innocent alike, to gods, to devils, to heaven and to the very depths of hell. I have wiped whole nations off the face of the earth and devastated their kingdoms. All at your bidding. I have followed generations to their graves and have stood by them, leaning on my dripping sword, resting until new generations have summoned me with their young, impatient voices. I have whipped thousands to death and silenced their restlessness for ever, I have burned prophets and redeemers as heretics, I have cast darkness and night over men's lives. All for you.

"They still call on me, and I obey. When I look out across the earth and see it burning and sweltering in its feverish heat, when I hear the sky echo with the screeching of sick birds of prey—then I know evil has once again come into its own, and the day of the executioner is come.

"I see the sun caught up in a stifling haze of cloud, and the light that seeps through is dim and thick, and evil. I go from field to field, abhorred and feared, and I reap my harvest. I wear the badge of the criminal on my forehead, for I am a criminal too, condemned to eternal punishment, because of you.

"I am condemned to serve you, and I serve you faithfully. The blood of centuries has been shed by my hands, and for your sake I have filled my very soul with blood. Your lust for blood overwhelms and blinds me, and the screams of your commands madden me and I run wild, wreaking death and destruction throughout the earth. I am a prisoner and you are my gaol. I cannot escape from you.

"When I look out through the darkened window of my home and see the beautiful meadows with their flowers and trees in the magnificent, peaceful stillness of the evening—then I feel stifled by my emptiness, my despair, and if I did not have her by my side I would collapse completely."

He looked at the poor woman who could have been a beggar, and their eyes met.

"I have to turn away, for I cannot bear to see that life can be so beautiful. But she stays by the window and looks out until dusk comes. We are fellow-prisoners; but though she is a captive like me, she can still look out upon the beauty of the earth, and she can live with it. She keeps our house clean and tidy, as if it were a normal home with ordinary people living in it. She lays a cloth on the table where I eat, and when darkness falls she strokes my forehead and tells me the gallows-mark is no longer there. She is like no other woman: she can love me. I do not know who she is, but she is good to me. I have asked men and women who she is, but nobody can tell me. Can you tell me why she looks after our home, or why she loves me?

"My home is an executioner's home, and I cannot bear the thought of changing it: when I think of that my terror overwhelms me even more.

"When she has fallen asleep in my arms I get up and put a blanket over her. Then I get ready, quietly, so that I shall not wake her. I steal away to my work at night, under a sky that hangs dark and threatening above the earth, and I am glad she is asleep; I am glad I am alone with the burden only I have to bear.

"But I know that when I come back from my work, bowed down under the weight of the blood that covers me, she will be waiting for me.

"Why must I suffer all this, all the horror and guilt you have created? Why must mankind's blood cry out from within me, and never leave me in peace? Why must the curses of the guilty and the sufferings of the innocent be heaped upon my miserable soul? Why?

"The condemned, poor wretches, plague me with their despair as they wait for their hour to come. I hate listening to them, but I cannot forget their pitiful cries. Voices from the far distant past cry out in me, voices nobody remembers, voices with no life but the life they live in me. The smell of the blood shed by man fills me with loathing, and weighs me down with a guilt that nothing can remove.

"Long, long after you have been laid to rest in your graves, long after your deeds have been forgotten, I shall still be carrying your burden, and I shall not fall by the wayside.

"But who can dig a grave deep enough to cover *me*? Who can relieve *me* of the curse I bear and grant me the peaceful release of death? Nobody: for there is nobody else who can suffer what I suffer.

"Once, hundreds of years ago, in the days when there was still a god, I went to him to ask him for help, to beg him to release me. What an answer he gave me!

"It all started, I remember, when I had to look after a man who said he was your saviour. He said he wanted to redeem you by suffering and dying for you. And he wanted to take my burden from me.

"I could not understand what he meant, for I could see he was a weakling without even the strength of a normal man, and I had to laugh at him. He called himself Messiah, and he had preached 'Peace on earth' and had been condemned for it.

"He told me that even as a child he had known that he was fated to suffer and die for mankind. He told me a lot about his childhood, as they all do. He talked about a country called Galilee and about how wonderful it was. They all say the same when their time draws near, and when this poor creature had been talking for a while, I realized that he was mad. He said the mountains were covered with lilies, and as he stood in the beautiful fields, with the mountains and flowers all around him, he realized he was the Son of God. He looked at the lilies and he knew what he was going to preach to mankind. His message to them was to be: 'Peace on earth'. I asked him why he had to die in order to give them peace, but he simply said he had to; he would not explain why. His father had said it would be so, and when he said his father he meant none other than God. He still had the faith of a good little child.

"But as his time drew near he began to fret and tremble like all the others, and he was no longer so sure of himself. I said nothing and he just sat there, thinking about what was to come. Now and again a far-away look seemed to come into his eyes, as if he were longing to be back in his childhood home, among the lilies in the fields.

"Then his fear turned to despair, and he fell on his knees and began to pray in a low voice: 'My soul is exceeding sorrowful, even unto death. O my Father, if it be possible, let this cup pass from me.' When the time came I had to take him out.

"He hardly had strength enough to carry the cross, and he staggered so pitiably under its weight that I took it and carried it for him for a time. No one else offered to do what I did, but then the cross made little difference to the weight I am used to carrying for mankind.

"I put him on the cross, and before I began I asked him to forgive me, as I always do. There was something, I cannot say what, but there was something about killing that man that hurt me. He looked up at me, and there was fear in those good, kind eyes. They were not the eyes of a criminal, but of a poor, unhappy, ordinary man. 'I forgive you, brother,' he said in his soft voice, and somebody who was standing near by told me the executioner's mark vanished as he spoke: but that I cannot believe.

"I cannot understand why he called me 'brother', but he did, and I felt that it really was my own brother I was crucifying. I did not want to look at him, but I had to from time to time, and for some mysterious reason he looked quite different from any of the others I have had to kill. Crucifying that man hurt me more than anything has ever done

"I shall never forget his eyes as he looked at me and said that. I remember it all so well, despite all the other voices and despite all the blood I have shed. But you forgot it generations ago: you remember none of the sins for which I have to suffer, or the guilt I alone have to bear.

"Before we set out from the prison I had to scourge him, and his body was swollen and sore: as if he could not die without that! When we reached the place where he was to be crucified I was so weary of it all that I could hardly set up the cross.

"But when I managed to raise it they were all so happy. They shouted and cheered when they saw him crucified at last: I have never seen such rejoicing at a place of execution. They mocked and jeered and reviled him, the poor man who thought he was their Messiah, their Christ. They shouted abuse at him and laughed at their own words, as they laughed at his suffering. He kept his eyes closed so that he should not see the people he was redeeming, and perhaps he was comforting himself with the thought that he was still their king, and still the Lord's anointed. They had made him a crown of thorns and it sat at a ridiculous angle on his bleeding head. The whole business was so sickening that I had to turn away.

"But before he gave up the ghost, darkness descended over the whole earth, and I heard him calling out in a loud voice: 'My God, my God, why hast thou forsaken me?' I could hardly bear to stay there any longer. Shortly afterwards he died a merciful death, and we took him down as quickly as we could, for the sabbath was approaching and his body could not be left on the cross.

"When everyone had gone away to prepare for the sabbath, and I was alone at last, I sat down in the midst of the filth and the stench of dead bodies that I am so used to. I sat there under the stars until long after midnight, and it was then that I decided I would go to speak with God.

"I left the earth and set out into the heavens, and as I walked away I felt free from the earth's stifling closeness. I walked on and on, I cannot say how far—but God lived a terribly long way away.

"At last I saw him, the high and mighty, sitting on his throne in the heavens before me. I walked up to him, stood before him and leaned my bloodstained axe against his throne. 'I am tired of my work,' I said. 'Have I not served for long enough? You must release me now!'

"But he just sat there, staring out into space, as motionless as a statue.

"'Listen to me! I have had enough, I cannot stand any more; I cannot live amidst the bloodshed and all the other horrors you permit. And why do you permit them, why? What is the sense of it all? I have done my work faithfully, I have done my utmost, but I cannot go on! I cannot stand it, I must stop, do you hear me?'

"But he would not look at me: he sat there looking out into space as if he were scanning the horizon of a desert, and there was an empty, far-away look in those great eyes. I was filled with terror, and with an unendurable despair.

"I became frantic, and screamed at him: 'Today I have crucified your own son!' But there was not a movement in that hard, unfeeling face: it was just like a lump of carved stone.

"I stood there in the cold and the silence, and I felt the wind of eternity piercing through me. There was nothing I could do, no one I could talk to: nothing. I took up my axe and went back the way I had come.

"I realized it was not his son I had crucified. He was just an ordinary man, and it was no wonder he had been treated as man has always treated man. They had simply had one of their own kind crucified, and there was nothing unusual about that. I was angry and shaken as I made my way along the cold road back.

"He had been taken away like all the others, and had been laid to rest. But I had to continue my wretched life as I had done before and as I shall have to until the end of time. I was simply driven back to earth to tread the path of pain and suffering again. There was nobody to free *me*.

"No, he was no saviour: how could he be? He had the hands of a mere boy, and driving the nails through them and those thin legs of his was a heart-rending business; I even wondered if they were strong enough to hold him up there. How could a man like that possibly be the redeemer of mankind?

"When I stuck my sword in his side to see when he could be taken down, he was already dead. He had died much sooner than they usually do. But what did that poor creature die for? How did he think he could help *you*? Or take my burden from me? What sort of Christ was he to try to save mankind? It was then that I realized why you need me to serve you, why you always call on me: because *I* am your Christ, I have been sent to you with the mark of the scaffold on my forehead, and I have my message to give you: strife on earth and ill will to all mankind!

"You have turned your god to stone, and he has been dead for centuries. But I, your Christ, I live on! I am my father's mighty thought, the son he conceived and sent to you when he was still alive and strong and knew what he wanted life on earth to be like! Now he's crumbling away on his throne like a leper, and the howling winds of eternity are casting his dust like ashes out into the wilderness of heaven. But your Christ lives on, 'so that ye may live'. I make my way through the world, and every day I redeem you with blood. But you don't crucify me!

"I am longing for death, just as my poor, helpless brother did. I am longing to be nailed to my cross and give up my spirit to the great, merciful darkness. But I know that day will never come. So long as you remain on earth I have to go on with my work; you will never make a cross for *me*. And when at last I have finished my work and there is nothing left for me to do here, I shall still be hunted like a restless phantom through the darkness of the heavens, the length and breadth of my father's great tomb, persecuted by my tormented soul and haunted by the memory of what I have done for you!

"But still I long for that day: I long for the end, for the

time when I shall no longer have to add to my great burden of guilt. I long for the day when you will be wiped off the face of the earth, and my arm will at last be allowed to rest. Then there will be no more voices crying out for blood. I shall be alone, I shall look around and know that my work is done. And then I shall make my way out into the darkness of eternity, trailing my axe behind me across the barren earth in memory of those who lived there."

He looked at them with his hard, burning eyes. Then he shot up from the table, strode angrily to the door, and was about to open it when the woman who had been sitting beside him, the woman who looked like a beggar, stood up and spoke to him. Her voice was calm and soft, and her whole face seemed to be shining with a strange, sorrowful happiness.

"I shall be waiting for you. You know that when you come home, weary, with blood on your hands, I shall be waiting there among the birches. You will rest your head in my lap, and I shall kiss your burning forehead and wash the blood from you. I shall be waiting, and I shall love you."

He looked at her, and his face wore a sad, peaceful smile. The sound of muffled drums came from outside and he stood and listened. Then he took a pull at his belt and went out into the cold, grey dawn.